LIE

Caroline Bock

St. Martin's Griffin ☙ New York

This is a work of fiction. All of the characters, organizations, and events portrayed in this novel are either products of the author's imagination or are used fictitiously.

www.stmartins.com

Book design by Gretchen Achilles

ISBN 978-0-312-66832-7

FIRST EDITION: SEPTEMBER 2011

10 9 8 7 6 5 4 3 2 1

To Richard

The attacks were such an established pastime that the youths, who have pleaded not guilty, had a casual and derogatory term for it, "beaner hopping."

—*The New York Times,* front-page story after
the murder of a Hispanic immigrant on Long Island

Skylar Thompson

I should be in calculus, reviewing for the final, not at the police station. Or I should be in the school parking lot, deciding on whether to cut class and go to the beach with the other seniors. Or at the diner with Lisa Marie. Or even home. I should be anywhere but here.

"Let me tell you about Jimmy," I answer Officer Healey. "Jimmy stands up for his friends, keeps his word, and is the star of the varsity football and baseball teams. He couldn't have planned to hurt any Mexicans. Especially brothers. Jimmy has a little brother." I've been here for over an hour, being asked about Jimmy, about last Saturday night. I sit up straighter. "And it's important for you to know that I've never called anyone a 'beaner,' and I've never heard Jimmy use that word either."

Officer Healey hunches over, slashes down notes, not disagreeing or agreeing. He has sprigs of red hair, watery eyes, and he winces as if thinking hard. He could be any of my friends' dads, a coach of soccer or Little League, a worrier, a sideline pacer.

"No one at school ever talked about going out and jumping Hispanics or other foreign nationals just for fun? No one used the term 'beaner-hopping'? No one said anything like that in school?"

I shift toward the edge of the metal chair to keep my balance. I wish I were taller. I run my hands through my hair. I should have brushed it back, worn something other than black, practiced smiling like Lisa Marie suggested.

"Anything more you want to tell me? Better to do it now, Miss Thompson."

He clears his throat.

"One more question. Was Jimmy Seeger the mastermind?"

My father shifts next to me. He's a big man and they've given him a wobbly chair. "Lookit, my daughter isn't a liar."

"Dad—"

"I'm just telling the officer you have nothing more to say."

Officer Healey stands as we stand. My father's chair crashes to the floor and breaks apart; he folds the pieces on top of the table like a broken body.

"Just so you know, the victim, Arturo Cortez, is in bad shape. He's in the ICU. If he dies, we charge your boyfriend with murder. As an adult. He's eighteen. One more time, is there anything you want to add?"

"What about the other brother I read about?"

"The younger brother, one Carlos Cortez, had minor injuries. He's the one that got their license plate. Bright kid. He's been released from the hospital."

"Lookit, if we're finished, we're finished," says my father, avoiding eye contact with either the police officer or me.

I hesitate. I have one more thing to ask. "When can I see Jimmy?"

"You're not," answers my father.

"His family's got to post bond," responds Officer Healey. "If not, the county jail allows twice-weekly one-hour visits. That's for nonattorneys."

"Two visits a week?"

"This isn't summer camp," says Officer Healey, squinting hard. "To visit, you got to be eighteen years old, with a valid ID, or be accompanied by an adult."

"Forgetaboutit," says my father. "The whole thing. Forget about it. Let's go."

"My birthday is this week, or should we 'forgetaboutit' too?"

He studies his scuffed-up work shoes.

"Any more questions?" asks the police officer hoarsely.

I will myself to say nothing. I have a million more questions racing through my head but I only shake my head. This was the plan. Everybody knows. Nobody's talking.

The officer follows us out to the main entrance. "If there's anything else you can think of, please give me a call. We appreciate your cooperation."

My father slips the card into his EMT uniform.

I know I will have nothing more to say.

From the top of the steps, Officer Healey watches us drive away. I ease my mother's car, a red Mustang, my car, through the choked police parking lot. *Mastermind* is racing through my head. Jimmy isn't that smart. I mean, he *is* smart—he was a Scholar-Athlete of the Year.

I drive slower than usual.

I don't know how it happened, last Saturday night. It wasn't supposed to happen. But all I have to do is say nothing and it will be Jimmy and me in the Mustang going east, going out to Montauk as planned. Say nothing; he'll be back.

My eyes lock in front of me. I estimate thirty, twenty, ten feet to go, and I'm free, except I'm going the wrong way.

"Make a right here," instructs my father. "A right. Your other right."

I make a sharp right to the exit of the police parking lot.

My father then starts in about food. Going to lunch at the

diner. Burgers and oversized onion rings. A vanilla milkshake, he ventures. Since it's Monday he doesn't have to be at work until four p.m. His insistence surprises me. We haven't been out to eat since my mother died. I shake my head at the diner suggestion. I want to get back to school and find Lisa Marie and tell her exactly what I said. Our hope is that Jimmy and Sean will be out on bail sooner than later. They were arrested on Sunday. Twenty-four hours without Jimmy is about as much as I can bear.

"You okay?" my father asks, not really wanting an answer.

So I answer him with a question. "You know I was there, Saturday night?"

"I don't want to know." He sighs. Adds to the space between us. "I don't need to know."

I jump the Mustang into traffic.

Sean Mayer
Jimmy's best friend

Are you okay? I ask myself for the hundredth time since being arrested.

Yes, I lie.

I have never been so alone as I am here, in a cell, with eight other guys. It's the right number for a baseball team. It even smells like feet and sweat and urine, like a locker room. But nobody's swinging a bat in here.

The cops separated Jimmy and me because he's eighteen. His last words were, "Stay strong."

Stay strong, and breathe. Breathe.

I can't. I'm afraid to shut my eyes on this bunk. I never liked closed-in places, tree houses, backs of buses. I like playing the outfield, center field. Fields of green grass.

I rattle out of the bunk in a cold sweat. Everybody is rumbling, roaring, running at the mouth, and it's about me, pitched at my back. How I'm scared. How I'm a boy. How I'm white. I have no issue with them, especially eight-on-one. I pretend they're the opposing team, testing me. I block out their noise like I always did. I clutch the metal bars. Somewhere cells are banged open or slammed shut, and the reverb drills into my hands and shoulders.

Breathe. Breathe. Remember the visualization exercises. The first time, last August, the football team all tumbled onto the gym mats after an endless practice in the sun. We were missing Richie Alan, who was supposed to be the quarterback, and who was my former best friend. His father had lost his job. They had to sell their house and leave for his grandmother's apartment somewhere in Queens, which might as well mean they moved off-planet.

We jokingly sat cross-legged and closed our eyes. When the coach asked us to "mentally rehearse," I cracked everyone up by saying, "I know what I'm mentally rehearsing." All I was really thinking was that I wanted to play ball, not think of the ball.

Then Jimmy spoke up. He said that he knew that we sucked last year. That if we really wanted to win, we should be open to trying this. Everyone looked at everyone else. We couldn't believe that Jimmy, the new guy, was saying this. But that was Jimmy, I'd learn.

"Let me try to get the guys through this. Coach?" The two new guys sized each other up, Jimmy and Coach Martinez. Jimmy had a way of standing with his shoulders back and hands clasped in front of him that I was already working on imitating. He was as tall as the coach, six-three or six-four. He could stand awesomely still. He did that with the coach. "I only want to help," he said to the coach. "I only want to win." Jimmy didn't even blink. After that practice, I stood in front of the mirror at home and practiced standing still and not blinking.

The coach saluted him, a mock salute, a go-ahead-you-try salute. We were all quiet, had stopped twisting in our gym shorts, picking at our zits. Eyes followed Jimmy.

"Listen up. We're going to breathe like the coach said," Jimmy shouted. "Breathe. Breathe." And we did. Until our breaths, heaves of air, were in sync with his, until we could see, like him, that winning was a possibility this season.

Now there are no images in my head except one. Of him. Arturo Cortez.

Breathe. Breathe.

What were you thinking of, Sean? What did you think you were doing? What did you imagine would happen, Sean? My father couldn't understand and I didn't help him out this time. I was covering Jimmy. I was running his plays. I wasn't thinking.

I press up against the bars like I'm in the weight room. Groan with the effort of lifting what can't be lifted. What happens in jail if you stop breathing?

Lisa Marie Murano
Skylar's best friend

"Listen up, I don't have a lot of time. You trust me?"

"Always."

"And, Lisa Marie?"

"Jimmy?" I murmur, even though I could easily scream out loud, announce to the world, that Jimmy is calling me from jail. I'm parked at the back of the diner lot. The Camaro is running; the air blasts. Even so, I can still smell the stink of fish from the diner's kitchen. When something smells that bad you can't escape. Feral black and white cats dash in front of my bumper as if crazed by possibilities.

"We don't have long to talk and I need you to—"

The time glows in the dark. At nine p.m., I'm supposed to meet Skylar at our other diner. It's almost nine. I don't mention this to Jimmy. Don't get me wrong. I don't mean for this to be a "lie of omission," as my father would say, which only means you know something and don't say it. I just don't want to make Jimmy feel bad that he isn't meeting up with us like always.

Yet, I have to ask, "Have you called Skylar too?"

"I'll call Skylar as soon as I can. Will you tell her?"

I'm mesmerized by the cats prowling, hunting down something.

"Are you there, Lisa Marie? I feel like everyone is falling away—"

"I'm here, Jimmy. I'm focused. I am."

A cat yowls.

"Good. I need you to be. You know Skylar can't handle this. I'm afraid. For her. She could do or say anything. Listen up, I need you to keep everyone together, especially her. Make sure everybody knows—"

"Everybody knows, nobody's talking," I whisper into my cell phone even though I'm alone. "That's our mantra."

"Our what?"

"Mantra."

"Our what?"

"Our cheer or call-out, though of course we're not saying this in the school halls. Mantra—" My chest tightens. I want his approval more than I've ever wanted anyone's in my life, and don't get me wrong, I'm not usually looking for anybody's approval.

Silence. I'm not sure what's wrong. He releases one of his deep, rolling laughs, and I breathe. "Speak English, L.M. That's the problem. Nobody speaks English anymore." He practically shouts this into the phone as if he's making sure others hear it. I focus on the "L.M." Only Jimmy calls me L.M. He gave me that nickname like a present, and already I miss it.

"Everybody knows, nobody's talking," I repeat firmly. I must keep everyone on the same page. We must hang together. It was a terrible mistake, what happened. It was supposed to be all in fun. I don't know what went wrong last Saturday night, none of us really do. But it can't be entirely Jimmy and Sean's fault. Jimmy can't be guilty of—he's not. Neither is Sean. They don't deserve this. They're my friends. That's what I keep telling myself.

Two cats track another cat. They dart across the parking lot, hissing at this third-scrawniest cat, one with yellow eyes.

"Lisa Marie, have you talked with your dad? Will he help me?"

"I haven't. But I will."

I wet my lips, dig for my lip gloss. Not for the first time, I think how different this past year would have been if Jimmy had met me without Skylar. Don't get me wrong, I am totally happy that Skylar has Jimmy. He's been there for her when she really needed someone.

"Lisa Marie?"

I jump in my skin. I'm here for him. He needs to know that I will always be there for him, no matter what, no matter if Skylar— No, I can't think of that. Skylar is going to remain true. I'm going to see to that.

"L.M?" he shouts into the phone. He wants me. He needs me. This isn't the first time, but I'm not going to think of that now. I'm going to stay focused.

"Jimmy—"

Right in front of my car, two cats pounce on that scrawny, yellow-eyed one for no reason I can see. This isn't fair, I think, honking my horn, sending them all careening into corners.

"Jimmy," I say, my heart pounding. "I'm here for you."

The diner. Not the one that smells like fish. But the King's Diner near the expressway, the L.I.E., with the neon and art deco booths and tabletop jukeboxes. That's our diner. Lisa Marie said to meet at the diner tonight. We didn't want to talk at school. No one is talking there. I'm here exactly on time. Nine p.m. I hate being late. That's the one way I'm like my father.

When Lisa Marie rushes in, forty-five minutes late, she slides into the booth next to me. Her embrace is fierce. I was waiting for that hug. She has news from her father, a lawyer. That's why she's late.

"Jimmy and Sean have been charged. With assault," says Lisa Marie, breathless. "Sean's parents are of course making bail tomorrow. I'm sorry."

My throat is dry. I need a glass of water. The diner is deserted of help. It's so late the King's Diner smells of cleaning supplies, of coffee grounds, of waitresses with cigarette smoke and perfume stuck in their hair—and I don't know what else. Maybe it'll rain tonight. My mother used to love a spring rain. This bountiful rain, she'd say, would help the flowers grow. Make the grass smell green, as if green were a smell.

It takes a moment for what Lisa Marie said to sink in. Sean's parents are making bail. Jimmy's are not.

"You sat up straight and looked them right in the eye, Skylar?"

Count the cars, speeding into the mist. Watch the windows fog with a breath. Jimmy, he loves the ocean in the rain. Nobody was on the beach when we drove out to Montauk that time in the torrential end-of-summer rain. Nobody except us. He said he wanted to kiss me for the first time where the air was the purest. He smelled like sea salt for a week afterward. So did I. Now I can't look at Lisa Marie.

"Skylar. You have to trust me."

"You know a lot of the diners are closing on Long Island. We used to have a half a dozen here. Jimmy says nothing is like it used to be. My father and mother always liked this diner the best; we ate here most Saturday nights. Maybe we should listen to some music? Remember how we cut school on Jimmy's birthday and banged in here ordering rounds of milkshakes? Last month. May first?"

Pink nails drill on the top of the fake red leather booth. When did Lisa Marie have time to get a manicure, or to put on makeup, or to buy what looks like a new pink sleeveless turtleneck, her arms sculpted from a winter of dedicated workouts?

I chew on my lips.

"Skylar. Focus. Jimmy is in the county jail and we don't know for how long. That doesn't seem fair at all. What did you say to the police? We all have to be saying the same thing. We have to trust one another to do this."

Don't trust me. Feel my pulse. Can't you tell my heart is breaking?

"Take your order, hon?" I recognize our waitress. She lives around the corner, is divorced, with two kids, grown up, must be in their twenties, living with her. Her hair is an unnatural yellow, her eyebrows overplucked and drawn back in. Her front teeth overlap. The smell of fried food swirls around her. Maybe she was cute in her day. Maybe she had her Jimmy and something went horribly wrong.

I'm staring. I know. I'm impolite. She shoots me a bitter smile. She knows me too.

"Sure," I say, pretending to study the oversized menu.

"Jimmy Seeger is a nice boy," she says. Her voice is wracked by cigarettes. "I know his mother. Works at Family Pharmacy. Goes to our church. Maybe nothing happened. Maybe it wasn't his fault. Self-defense. We're being overrun. I give them boys a lot of credit for doing something about it. No one else will." She hacks, doubles over, before straightening up and smiling at us. "What can I get you, girls?"

I order eggs over easy, whole wheat toast. A vanilla milkshake. My diner standard. On top of everything, I'm going to get fat.

"Why hasn't Jimmy called me yet?"

Lisa Marie grasps each of my hands in her own. "He will."

"I need to hear his voice." It hurts, physically hurts, in the pit of my stomach, to say how much.

"I know. He'll call as soon as he can, I'm sure."

I squeeze her hands back. We hold on to one another until the eggs arrive smelling like eggs and grease. I can't eat.

"What did you say, Skylar? To the police?"

It was all a mistake. If he had known that they were brothers this never would have happened. A mistake. But I didn't say that.

My father said that the one in the hospital would most likely be out of there before Jimmy is out on bail. Those people, he said, are used to much more physical activity than any of us. They need to get back to work, so they rebound quicker. A few punches from some high school kids are not going to kill someone like that, he added. *A few punches.*

I need to see Jimmy. I need to hear his voice. To know he's

okay. To hear him tell me I'm okay. To hold me like no one else can. And I'm sure he needs to know that I am here for him, will always be, that his plan for next year is still on, that we are going to take a year off, sail from Montauk to Florida on his grandmother's boat, and leave this behind.

A mistake. I wasn't there, that's what I told the police. That should be the end of what I have to say. I wasn't there. Three words. Nobody knows I was except my father and Lisa Marie. A lie. Even so, sometimes it's worse to tell people the truth even if they say they want to hear it. Mothers die. And you have to live with what you say for the rest of your life. With the mistake of telling what you think is the truth. The truth lies. The truth is—

"Focus. Skylar. Focus. We're all in this together," says Lisa Marie, too brightly for me. "You chose Jimmy's side a long time ago, didn't you? Didn't you choose his side?"

I tear my toast in half, then in quarters, then in even eighths, and sixteenths, keeping track mathematically, keeping sane. "Why is Sean getting out on bail but not Jimmy?"

"You know why Jimmy isn't out on bail?" She sips her usual: black coffee. "He isn't out on bail because his family couldn't afford it. That's what my father says. They found money for a law-yer but not bail. And I'm sure you're worried about Jimmy. I am too. I'm worried about Jimmy. And Sean too." She pauses until I look at her. "They need us to survive this."

Jimmy's father has been on disability ever since 9/11. He doesn't even own the house they live in. Their family moved in last August, coming closer to the city from Montauk. Their house is old. It leans up against the Long Island Railroad tracks. Jimmy hates that house. He says he can tell the time by the trains. They sound like they're barreling through his bedroom. Jimmy always said only the very rich or the very poor can live in Montauk anymore, that's why his parents moved here.

I met him a month after my mother died.

He doesn't even have his own car.

"Did you look like that when you talked with the police?" Lisa Marie is scrutinizing me.

A black T-shirt swims on me. My arms are skinny and shapeless. I'm wearing black spandex leggings. I've lost at least twenty pounds since my mother died and my father started working double shifts. We both forget to grocery-shop. I drop my head. Hairs fly across my sight.

Lisa Marie continues while I'm imploding. "I wore a sleeveless chartreuse sundress when I met with the police. Everyone was looking at me. I thought it would be like one of those police shows where they play good cop/bad cop and one of them is really mean and the other tries to sweet-talk you. It wasn't like that. They just believed every word I said."

I stuff a piece of toast into my mouth and chew and gag.

"Did you know that those two brothers weren't from Mexico?" Lisa Marie is saying this over her cup of coffee. Her eyes glisten. She has taken to wearing fake eyelashes. "They're from El Salvador."

"Where's that?" I am geographically challenged. Math is my subject, though I don't know what I'll do with it. Teach, maybe.

"Far from here. Does it matter? El Salvador. Mexico. They're not from here. Focus on what matters. On Jimmy. On Sean."

Here is its own world. Many people brought up here never leave—like my father—or come back to raise their families after

15

living somewhere else. That's what my mom did after going to college in Boston. And everyone who works in Manhattan takes the same train home every day. Here is school. I have never been smart enough for the real brains even though I have always been in most of their classes. I have never been a cheerleader. I have never been into sports, never a girl jock. I have never been in the band. Instead, I live in that land of in-between, floating—at least that's the way it was before I met Jimmy. I went to nursery school with most of the people in my high school class. Sean and Lisa Marie live on my block. I've known Lisa Marie since I was in second grade and she in first. Maybe she was never the top student in her class—I definitely helped her with geometry and algebra along the way—but she gives her total attention to whatever she decides needs it: the annual blood drive, her friends, me. She was my best friend when no one else was. But everything changed for me here, for all of us, when Jimmy moved to our town last summer.

I gulp from my glass of clouded water. If I don't die from grief the diner water will do it.

Lisa Marie is looking at me strange.

"Does your father think Jimmy is going to have to stay in jail?" I ask.

"Unless his family can make bail for him."

"Or until there's some kind of trial?" I ask, panicky.

"Yes. Or unless they cut a deal."

"A deal?"

"Skylar. Please, focus. There could be a trial. Or they could make some kind of a special arrangement—that's a 'deal.'"

"What kind?"

"Skylar! This is what happens when you plead not guilty."

"Not guilty?"

"Not guilty. Remember, Skylar. Not guilty. There's nothing more to say after that. Not guilty."

I want to say more, but I know Lisa Marie doesn't want to hear me hurtle on about Jimmy, about that night, the incident, the idea that people could think, are thinking, that we are some kind of horrible group of kids—and we aren't. That's the truth.

Lisa Marie clamps pink nails into my wrists. I can smell mint mouthwash on her breath. "None of us are guilty. Remember that. Keep saying that. Say it now."

If I open my mouth, I could say that. I tilt my head back. I'm dizzy with what I could say.

"Are you okay?" Lisa Marie asks, close and far away at the same time, a blur.

"Yes," I lie.

Everybody knew.

No one told.

I swoop around the bend into the heart of the neighborhood, toward my house, gunning my Camaro. High leafy trees blow shadows. Empty streets narrow. It's like I'm the only one alive.

What did everyone know? That Jimmy and Sean and a rotating, roving band of a dozen other seniors went beaner-hopping every Saturday night for months. It was just play, it was fun, it was nothing—at first. Jimmy was funny about it, saying how they had to go out on patrol, how they had to hunt them down and chase them off our land, how it was like a video game but more. He was protecting us all. For once, something was exciting in our lives. Thing is, Jimmy is a natural-born leader. He's going to be a general or a president of something big. I'm trying to be very analytical about all this, very unemotional. I have to be. Especially since I promised Jimmy I would be.

Thing is, the police are asking us all to voluntarily give statements. No one is talking. I mean, Skylar and I talked to the police, but we didn't say anything. At least, I'm sure I didn't.

But like I said. Everybody knew.

Skylar understands this. As Jimmy's girl, and my friend, she'd better be smart enough to know this. I mean, I know she's smart, but Skylar can be really dumb. Don't get me wrong, we've been friends since I moved in across the street from her in first grade. She was in second grade, the older sister I always wanted to have, even with her flyaway, in between blond and brown rolls of hair that she'd never do anything about except bunch up on the back of her neck. In my case, I've been a perfect blond ever since I could say, "Hair salon, Mommy."

When her mother died of ovarian cancer, I was the first one at her house, engulfing her in a world-class Lisa Marie hug, offering to help, urging her to talk about her mother's passing. All she said was that her mother didn't "pass," she "died." I'm thinking of being either a psychologist or a fashion stylist, I haven't decided which one, but I could have helped her more if she had let me. Some people, like my mother, wonder why I stay friends with her. It's impossible for me not to stay friends with Skylar. That's the kind of person I am. Loyal to my friends.

How did Jimmy and Skylar get together? It was after her mother died, last summer. Skylar wouldn't leave her house except for the funeral. I had to beg her that August night to come with me to Jake's pool party.

She had spent the whole summer inside and was ghostly scary pale, thin, with hair strung down her back, unwashed. To the party, she wore a thick black sweater, but I didn't say anything. Sometimes those parties were so crowded nobody went—you know what I mean, nobody who was anybody.

But that summer night, in August, I went because of her, and Jimmy was there with Sean. Jimmy was new to town. He had his hair cut short like he was a Marine already. He wore a buff polo shirt, didn't slouch or give out goofy smiles like Sean in his sweat-stained baseball tee. And of all people, Jimmy decided Skylar was interesting. He even used that word.

I was never sure what Jimmy meant by *interesting*. Don't get me wrong, I was thrilled when Jimmy and Skylar started going together. She needed someone to talk to. For some reason, that someone wasn't me, and Jimmy is a very intense listener with those magnetically blue eyes. His eyes turn on when someone is talking to him and you feel like you're the only person in the world with him. He saved her from herself.

Within a few weeks of that party, Jimmy turned Skylar's life around. She washed her hair, at least from what I saw. And her father let her do anything she wanted, and all she wanted was to be around Jimmy. At least that was normal. And that's what I wanted for Skylar with all my heart—I wanted her to stop sleep-walking through life. Jimmy was action and ideas and he made us feel like we all had a reason to go to school every day.

I have never thought of myself as naive, but have I been naive about Jimmy?

Absolutely not, I instantly decide.

Jimmy is perfect in a way I thought a guy could never be: funny and serious, great at sports and good in class. He gets along with everybody, with teachers and parents. He is plain gorgeous. Don't get me wrong, I know he is devoted to Skylar.

Ever since Jimmy and Sean were arrested on Sunday, Skylar's been manic. It's now Monday night. She has to calm down. She has to understand that this is life and death, or I am not going to be her friend. No one will be her friend if she tells the police anything.

I back into my driveway. I beat Skylar home. Across the street, her house has no lights on: none above her single-car garage, or in her one bathroom, or her little, lonely bedroom, or her father's. Nothing is remodeled, renovated, or updated in that house. Even the grass, tufts and scruff, is more brown than green. It's embarrassing. I see the bulky outline of Skylar's dad in their kitchen, in the dark.

When my dog, Treasure, died, my mother let me grieve for one day and at the end of the day she said that was enough, time to go on.

I watch Skylar's house for a moment more. I know she drives as slow as anything, but where is she?

The wind rises. Treetops shiver, swish against electric wires. Whiffs of popcorn float in the air, most likely from Sean's house, next to Skylar's. His mother always makes popcorn when she's upset, or when she's not. I take a deep breath, no calories in breathing.

Since I can't wait for her all night, I go inside my own well-lit house. I stop at my parents' bedroom. My father, a slight man, snores loudly on top of the bed, wearing his Yankees pajamas. The flat-screen blares the Yankees game. They're beating the Indians 2–0.

On Sunday, my father laughed when he heard about beaner-hopping, the boys' weekend pursuits, and said that they were amateurs. My father has a sick sense of humor. "Normally the cops out here don't even book kids like that. They'd go with a slap on their wrists. The police don't want to ruin these kids' lives by arresting them. And those people never file charges 'cause they're illegal. They don't want trouble. They should have been fast and run." I thought he was talking about the Mexicans, but he meant Jimmy and Sean. My father's a lawyer but not a very good one according to my mother, or at least not a very rich one.

Tonight, my mother has to wander out from her bathroom, wet. Her wispy white bathrobe is strung across her thin hips. "I need another sleeping pill." She shakes out two from a bottle on her nightstand next to a glass of white wine.

"Isn't it horrible, angel? How could those kids do that? Beat up someone they didn't even know? What was his name again?" She washes down her pills with wine.

I don't want to say his name.

"How could Sean be a part of this?"

"He wasn't. Not really."

"There was the boy's brother. He must have seen something. What are their names again? Martinez?"

"That's the coach's name, Mom."

She fluffs her short streaked blond hair. "More importantly, what did Skylar say to the police?"

"Nothing. She doesn't know anything, Mom."

"You're sure? Both of you girls have your whole lives ahead of you. I watched you grow up, well, not exactly together. Her mother was a little weird, and Skylar is like that too, isn't she? The fact that she never had a best friend her own age, that she always depended on you, I should have said something to her mother years ago. But none of this matters, except you, angel. I don't want any of this to hurt you. I don't want any guilt by association. You knew nothing about this as far as I know. You were at a party."

Protecting your friends doesn't make you guilty, does it? Does it? I don't feel guilty at all.

"I was at a party." I look straight into her bloodshot eyes. "At Skylar's," I add, though it was hardly a party. We didn't even go inside her house. It was just Skylar and me sending off Jimmy and Sean—they were going to do their thing.

"You don't drink. You don't do drugs. How do things like this happen? Some people in town are saying that those Hispanics provoked the fight when Jimmy and Sean were only offering to give them a ride. Though why would they do that? Offer men like that a ride? And what's this about beany-hopping? Did you ever hear of such a thing?"

"Beany-hopping, Mom?" I smile at her slurry translation. "Never."

She whirs at me, close up to me. Her breath is fruity and stale. "Isn't Arturo Cortez his name? The one in ICU? I hope he's okay— you wouldn't want this whole thing to be a bigger deal." She finishes off her wine. I wish I could taste some. Take a pill too. I don't want to think anymore.

"It's horrible, angel. What kind of town will people think we live in?"

What people? The only people that matter, to me, live here.

"Arturo Cortez is his name, isn't it?" she insists in the way she does when she drinks too much. She yanks down the snow-white blankets on her side of the big bed.

"I don't know." We called them "beaners."

"Is there something you want to tell me, just to get it off your chest? It won't go farther than this bedroom. I won't even tell your father." She catches my hand. Tugs my palm to her cheek. Her skin is clammy and cold.

Everybody knew.

Nobody told.

"Nothing, Mom. I mean, no, Mom, listen to me, I've told you all I know."

"Have you?" she says, closing her eyes. "I don't believe you."

Tommy Thompson
Skylar's father

I work for the city as an EMT. Skylar and I can afford to live here because Renee's mother and father willed us the house. Lookit, even now I never would have been able to buy into this neighborhood on my salary.

Renee's parents were the original owners. They did their thirty years and paid off the mortgage. I don't have to refinance or borrow from relatives or add an illegal apartment to make my monthly nut like so many of my neighbors.

I'm standing here in the dark, staring out the front picture window and thinking about my neighbors.

Some are doing fine. Some are living the lives we thought we'd have out here. From the outside you never know which ones aren't. A lot of people still have gardeners around here, like Skylar's friend, Lisa Marie, across the street. A Mexican with a mower, and one-two-three the lawn is cut. Me, I like to take care of my own lawn. Good exercise, and I can save a few bucks.

My in-laws bought in here when there were still potato fields around. My father-in-law was a World War II veteran, grew up in a tenement, and bought this house with a VA mortgage. Sure, the developer back then was only selling to whites. Didn't matter if a black man was also a veteran. We didn't have any Hispanics to deal with back then. Maybe it's better if they have their towns and we have ours.

I don't know if it's like this everywhere, but that's how it is here. Not that I have anything against anybody. Lookit, I work for the city. EMT. I work with all kinds and get along with every-body. And I'm doing nothing much but working these days. I'm killing myself to send Skylar to Boston College, where her mother went to school. Her mother, my wife, Renee, may she rest in peace, and I always wanted the best for Skylar. If her mother were still alive, she'd know what advice to give.

At least Skylar wasn't in the car with that moron last Saturday. She swears she wasn't in *his* car that night. That's all I asked her. I don't want to know anything else. I was at work, so I don't know where she was, but she has never lied to her mother—or to me. That's what I told the police.

Nobody's saying that she needs a lawyer, and why should she? She wasn't there as far as anybody's concerned. She doesn't know anything. She's not saying any more. Sure, I feel sorry for the kid in the hospital. Nobody should get beat up like that. But if my daugh-ter says she had nothing to do with it, she had nothing to do with it.

Lookit, I don't know about Jimmy. He was always trying to make conversation with me about I don't know what. Last week, maybe Friday—without Renee the days all run together, but it must have been Friday because Jimmy was here—we were having a perfectly fine conversation about nothing, about the Mets, my team, and he started railing about his coach. This got him onto all the illegals, the guys in those padded flannel shirts, at the Dis-count Mart near the L.I.E. looking for work every morning. How they should all be rounded up, shipped off. I didn't agree or dis-agree with him. All I wanted to do was sit my ass in my chair and watch the game. He looked at me and I know what he saw: a guy with a big gut, with more hair sticking out of his ears than on his head.

Maybe Jimmy had a point, but I'm not one to look for trouble. He said we had to defend our way of life. I said I defended it every day by going to work.

He wasn't against legal immigration. I asked him how his family got here, or were they American Indians? He said that his mother's family owned farmland out on the South Fork going back to the 1700s. He said his family documents are in Dutch, which is who were in charge here before the English. I said good for him. You can give history lessons. My father's father lied about his age and came over steerage, on his knees the whole way. He was called the Big Swede. What about giving these people a chance?

He said they were stealing our jobs. I said they were doing jobs nobody else wanted.

"You want them living next door to you? Twenty, thirty, or more Mexicans jammed in a house together?"

I don't want them living next door to me, he got me on that.

"What about Skylar's future?"

Skylar had edged into the living room. I wished we had a bigger house at that moment. But got to admit, Skylar and Jimmy looked right together. He slipped his hand against her hip. She leaned in to him, looking so much like her mother that my chest constricted. My pulse jumped. I had to sit down, but it was better to stand and look like a concerned father, nodding my head, not saying anything, concentrating on standing up.

Everybody bleeds red. That's what my partner always says as we're trying to keep some punk or skank or slob alive. I just don't want them bleeding on my lawn or on my daughter. But I didn't say that; I was flat-out exhausted. I let Jimmy have the last word.

And lookit, he's a persuasive guy, Jimmy is. Good-looking too.

I used to be good-looking like that—had the girls too—but it only got me thinking that I didn't have to pay attention to the law like other people. My sin was fast cars. Drag races down the L.I.E. Now I drive an ambulance for the city. Go figure.

But I wish I knew how to talk with Skylar. Last week—I don't know what day—she was going out and it was late, past ten. I was stumbling in after a double shift. I tried to speak with her. I didn't want her to go. I wanted her in the house with me. I wanted her to be a little girl again and run into my arms, instead of staring at me with those big hazel-green eyes like I was the world's biggest loser of a father.

For the first time in many dark months, I wanted to do something normal like go to the movies or to the diner. A child thinks a father is only a father, but we're our mix of memories, hopes, desires. She thinks only she can claim those things. All I could think was: This sucks.

Skylar asked me for money like always. I grunted, straining for my wallet, a zombie. I forced myself to say like any normal father, "Where are you going? It's late."

"I'm meeting up with Jimmy and everybody."

She plucked a twenty from my hand. I knew there was more to her plans. There had to be. Where were they going? With who exactly? These are the questions any normal father asks his teenage daughter, right? Not that any of that matters now. A kid is in the hospital, dying. I wish I had said, *Stop. Think about what you're doing. Think about the future. Think that I love you, and that is the greatest thing I can give you: more than money, or your friends, is the security of your father and mother's love.* But when I opened my mouth, all I said was, "Be careful with your mother's car."

"It's mine now, remember?" was all she said, and left me sunk in my chair.

That's where I go now, into my chair, like a slug. I'm thinking I can catch Skylar before she goes to bed and we can talk. I see Lisa Marie pull into her driveway.

And lookit, soon the fat, bald guy will be asleep like a dead man in the chair.

Skylar Thompson

I'm waiting for Jimmy to call, for Sean to come home, which is supposed to happen sometime around four p.m. according to Lisa Marie. Or for the world to end, as I drift from one airless room to another. I push open a kitchen window. It doesn't help. A screen falls off.

I wonder if I can miss the rest of school—all three weeks—and still graduate. I never thought senior year would be like this.

Last night, I came home late, very late. Where was I? Nowhere. Let's leave it at that. Nowhere.

All I'm saying is that Lisa Marie started all this. Last August, she insisted that I go to Jake Kroll's party. She said I had to go. Everybody wanted to see that I was alive. I wasn't. Not really. It had only been a month since my mother died.

That night Lisa Marie made me get dressed. I wore my black one-piece bathing suit, T-shirt and shorts over it. Everything hung on me. My legs were ghostly white. I hadn't been to the beach all summer. I grabbed my mother's sweater, her black one, just in case. It was steamy, over eighty degrees, and past ten o'clock. I hadn't been out of the house in weeks.

Jake's deck was packed. Everyone slouched at the railing, checking for anyone more interesting to come through the high white fence. I wasn't that person. Rap music pounded. The pool, one level down, with its slide that we were all jealous of as kids, glowed in colored lights. Rays of chlorine shot up.

Jake looked like he should be working a carnival. He jumped on a bench, wearing a Hawaiian shirt, barking out names, tossing beers, and promising that there was more to come. I wasn't into "more to come." That's what made Jake popular. He somehow got the "more" drinks or drugs than anyone else, and shared.

Lisa Marie marched us around the deck, swooped down the stairs, around the brick patio and empty pool that would be filled by midnight with drunken high school kids and the police would be called but I'd be long gone by then. She was annoyed. No one was there, nobody that counted.

Voices were snapping: *How ya doin'? How ya doin'? How ya' doin', Sky-larrrr?* My name sounded foreign. It was someone else's name. Someone who knew that "How ya doin'?" wasn't a question, that "How ya doin'?" didn't require an answer. Nobody wanted an answer. It was something to say. But I wanted to answer it. I wanted to say that I was not doing well, thank you. Not one of you called me after my mother's funeral. No one except Lisa Marie.

I scraped behind her, around the pool. When I looked up, she was hitting Sean in the forearm, saying that we expected to see him sooner, what did he think of Jake Kroll's party this year, and who was this?

"Jimmy Seeger." He offered his hand out to me as if I would shake it, then turned his palm up to show me he meant me no harm when I was too embarrassed to make contact. His hand was twice the size of my own. He was over six feet tall in a white polo shirt and Army greens. "What do you think of this party, of them?" He pointed to a group encircling Jake Kroll, chugging beers to the beat. "I hate rap."

"Me too," said Sean. I was shocked at him saying this. Shocked more when Sean yanked Lisa Marie away, hurrying off to see about other music, leaving me alone with Jimmy at the edge of the pool, feeling afraid and cold. Yet Jimmy's eyes fixed on me. He was seriously paying attention to me, even as everyone was paying attention to him, which even then thrilled me. My chest contracted. Or maybe what I remember is my seventeen-year-old heart stopped by the beauty of him, by his stature, by my effort to look up into his eyes and remain there because he wanted me to.

"I've heard from Sean that you've been through a lot," said Jimmy directly.

Enough space remained between us that he could step forward even as I was shivering, my arms lost in my mother's black sweater. "I'm sorry about your loss," he said, his eyes dwelling on mine. I felt as if I had been found.

"Listen," he said.

I felt I could hear his heartbeat or he could hear mine.

"Listen," he whispered. A bird frantically chirped from the far side of the pool. We'd go to it. Jimmy would untangle string from its chestnut wings, free it, save it.

It feels very important to remember details: the burn of chlorine; the brick set out in a swirling pattern, like there was movement in stone underneath my feet; the first sight of Jimmy: the bluest of blue, deep in his eyes.

I blink hard.

He has to call. Soon.

I race through the house, beating up all the windows for air, and find none. I crash toward the front kitchen with its dangling screen, and as if I'm choking, swat air toward me. Everybody knew what was going on. I knew. The bird. I should have told the police about that bird.

That night I met Jimmy, Jake Kroll leaped off the deck, pretending he could fly, and landed facedown on brick. He was scraped and bruised, but too drunk to be really hurt. Cheers split the crowd into those that encouraged Jake to fly again, and others who, I imagine, only wanted to hear themselves scream. Jimmy just surveyed all as if he were the adult and they were all children. Even now I can remember thinking: I'm glad he's not joining in taunting Jake. I knew that if he walked away right then, if I never hung out with Jimmy again, this was nice, this was good, this was enough. For the first time in a long time, since my mother died and even before that when she was sick for the entire spring of my junior year, unable to rise out of bed, or even, at the end, to feed herself, I didn't feel alone. A singular digit. A one. I didn't need more, or so I thought. Maybe I should have left that night and said that was enough and meant it. Yet last summer, we were all waiting for something more to happen, for the summer to end, for senior year to begin. Nothing happened until Jimmy got here.

At the party, the music changed. To what, I don't remember. But Jimmy said to me, *Good. Good. I like that song.*

A single note held, beckoned, fluttered.

My heart did too.

All the guys are triple-parked in front of my house. As soon as they spot me and my dad maneuvering down the street in his clanking, ten-year-old minivan they start a racket, honking, cheering, whistling. Lisa Marie drags me out of the van, cinches on to my arm like I don't know which way to go, and in a way I don't. She hugs me. She's thrilled. She's planned everything.

Then everyone is there, sticking their hands out to me. Jimmy had started that, the hand-shaking. With his huge hands and super grip, that's how he'd greet you. Everybody wanted to be friends with Jimmy. There was nothing better than him clasping your hand on your way to gym, or lunch. He'd boom out your name like he was announcing you had a place in the world that mattered and that place was right beside him.

But this afternoon, I don't take anybody's hand.

Lisa Marie goes off to greet a carload of guys from the baseball team. They're the loudest, hanging out of their SUV, the same kind of car that Jimmy and I were in last Saturday night, except a different color. The car I drove that night was mine. I don't know how Jimmy, or me, were ever friends with these guys except I've known them all my life, inherited them at birth.

Everyone wants to know how Jimmy is.

Someone suggests cutting school and driving out to the jail and waving to him from the parking lot. In June, it's a tradition for seniors to cut and go down to the town beach. Not jail.

I want to say, *You don't know what it's like.* I've always hated small spaces. It was like someone had shoved me into a box for forty-eight hours. I need to be outside. Sky and grass.

I shout out, "Jimmy is great. He's staying strong." That seems to be enough. A half dozen cars honk, speed off.

I don't know if Jimmy's "great" or "staying strong." In the police station, he said for me to "stay strong." He said it like a warning, as he was being led one way and me another.

My father and I are alone on the front lawn. Once, last week, he'd have swung his arm around me, and we'd have gone inside like that. Now my father, exhausted, says, "Five minutes and I want you in the house," and turns, leaves.

I know I should wait out here for Lisa Marie, say something to her, like thanks. I can't take too much of her, though. She's always hanging on any senior in a varsity jacket. Not me, of course. Everyone knows that she gives out BJs in her Camaro on a regular basis, or at least that's what all the guys on the team say. Even Jimmy must have been with her.

I don't think I could ever do anything with Lisa Marie, or, I guess, Skylar. It'd be like kissing one of my sisters, and I have four. Though, I got to say, Jimmy was obsessed with Skylar.

Jimmy used to call or text her every fifteen minutes or so. If she didn't respond, he'd go nuts, calling her every ten minutes, every five minutes, and it would be that she was taking a chemistry test or brushing her teeth. But even more—about a month ago, he told me that he couldn't sleep without her. He was staying with her on nights that her father worked and sleeping with her. Sleeping. Doing nothing but kissing. He said it was him making that decision. He could control himself. She was too fragile, still recovering from the death of her mother.

So I kidded him. Said, "What do you do on the nights her father doesn't work? Jack off all night? Call up Lisa Marie?" He wouldn't let me in on the weekend activities after that remark. He said I was frozen out for insubordination.

I had to beg him to give me another chance, saying I would down at least two beaners in his honor. Jimmy kept score on those things. He said what he cared about more was Skylar, protecting her, saving her from the hurts and ravages of the world. He added that to the reasons we went out to bean Mexicans, and I was back in. I was pumped. I was indestructible. For a while, Jimmy called us "the protectors." All the guys liked that.

I wish I felt some of those superpowers now. I've failed at everything. Failed Jimmy. And failed everyone else too.

I glance up and down the street for Lisa Marie or the SUV she left in. I don't blame them. I don't even want to be with me.

I failed Jimmy because I wore an old team jersey that night. Grass-stained, gray, faded; it helped identify us. I didn't even think they could read English. I didn't think. Even more. I failed Jimmy because he said, "go after the other one." And I didn't. He was fast. Or at least faster than me.

I'm sure Jimmy thinks I'm a loser. For him it's like being marked for life, deformed, diseased. I'm sure everybody thinks that I'm a loser, my parents, Lisa Marie, Skylar, everyone.

I fill up my lungs. The grass is spring-green here. I want to lie down and stare up through the trees and have the sound of nothing take over the sound of their voices: English, Spanish, screams without words, locked in my head. I didn't think. I watched. I watched someone being bashed and beat and—

I know I should be thinking now about a lot of other things:

what's going to happen next with me, with Jimmy. But in the middle of my front lawn, where I've lived all my life, and thrown a thousand balls to my father, and kicked up grass and dirt, and met my friends for game after game, all I can think of is how alone I am, and nobody's ever accused me of thinking too much.

And then, there she is at the edge of her lawn, next to my lawn, ours green, hers brown, Skylar, swaying. I ease over to her. I expect her to ask about Jimmy like the others. Except he's probably called her. She probably knows more than me.

All year, our conversations had revolved around Jimmy, comparing notes about what he said, what plans he had for the weekend, for the future, for us. Though we never talked about the outings, the beaner-hopping, as anything more than a game, did we? We talked about how lucky we were for Jimmy to have moved here. How the teachers, except the coach, the new one, loved him, and even so, Jimmy was the best at football, at baseball.

Skylar. She shifts side to side, a restless barefoot dance. "Did you say anything?" she whispers to me.

"You didn't, " I say, rousing myself, "did you?"

"Of course I didn't. But we need to talk. You and me. Sean. I can't stop thinking about what happened, can you? Sean?" She touches my forearm, lightly, as if she or I could float away. "Nobody is talking about anything but Jimmy and you. Nobody is talking about that night, I mean. It's like it happened but not because of us. And I keep thinking, what should we think? What should we say to ourselves? I'm not saying any of us confess to anything, but you, me, Jimmy have to talk about this. What are you thinking, Sean? What do you think Jimmy is thinking—"

"I don't know," I cut her off.

"I'm going to visit him."

"When?"

"Tomorrow."

"Tomorrow?"

"I don't know how else I'd celebrate my eighteenth birthday."

I dig my sneakers into her lawn. How can I ever face Jimmy again? I failed him. I failed. It was a test. He may not have called it that. He may have liked the more military terms, but I know it was a test. And I failed. I'm nothing. Maybe I never really believed that shit. That I was. A winner.

"Sean?"

I kick up a pocketful of mud. Punt it into the air. It explodes. "Happy birthday."

"What are you going to say?" she whispers. "What should I say, I mean, to Jimmy?"

The trees around us rustle as if in response. The evening light is pulled down the block. I have no more words for her, or me.

"Nobody is saying anything," says Lisa Marie, sweeping us up from behind, throwing her arms around both of us. "Don't think too much." I don't know if she means Skylar or me. Anyway, Lisa Marie is right. Nobody is saying anything.

Lisa Marie pats my cheek. "We all missed you. But it's time for you to go inside your house and reassure your mother and father. I'm going home now too." She kisses me on both cheeks. Nothing kisses. That's new. She does the same to Skylar and crosses the street to her house like everything is under control instead of madly spinning into space.

Skylar stays.

We say nothing else to one another for a long time.

And then I go into my house, into my room smelling of lemons, open the windows wide, and lie on my bed in the dark, thinking about nothing as hard as I can.

Mom cleaned, dusted like I was away at camp. My baseball uniform hangs in my closet ready for the game on Sunday. She's scrubbed the grass stains out. Jeans and a new polo are folded on my chair. I'd never admit it, but until this year she'd always laid out my clothes.

From the first, my mother thought Jimmy was a good influence. He wouldn't hang with anyone who wore graphic T-shirts or T-shirts in general. No earrings or chains or jewelry of any kind. No long hair. Mom was thrilled. He was going military, Army Rangers or Navy SEALs. I was going with him, after college.

Unlike Jimmy, I have to go to college. My mother would kill me if I didn't. She's still working on the coach to write a recommendation for me to the University of Florida so I can have an easier time as a walk-on to the baseball team. *How does anyone write a recommendation for me now? What do you write? Don't think. Think of nothing. Sleep.*

I've only been gone two days, from Sunday afternoon to today, Tuesday, but I feel like one Sean was arrested and another released. The new Sean looks the same, but is now thinking of things he never had to think of before: of what makes him hurt.

My bed smells like new sheets, not like other men's sweat. My blanket, my soft blue and green plaid blanket, is here. I pull it around me and try to clear my mind.

Except I can't think about nothing. My mind wanders back to the day Skylar met Jimmy. It all happened before I knew it was happening. She and Jimmy walked off, discovered this bird, an ordinary bird, maybe a sparrow, on the ground caught in some string, and he untangled it. The bird hopped off, flew a bit, even. Skylar called him her hero for saving that little brown bird. How can a guy who does that also plan to do what we did?

That night, Skylar said she wouldn't stay long. I couldn't blame her. Her mother had been dead maybe a month. He'd later say to me that he first noticed her legs, pale white in the shadows. Her mane of hair reminded him of a golden foal. I had to ask him what that was, and he said, "A horse, a baby horse." I thought: Skylar's not going to like being compared to a horse. She's more birdlike anyway. But I didn't go around labeling people as animals or vegetables like Jimmy did. I would never have come up with "beaners" for the Mexicans. But I didn't think anything was wrong with it. I thought it was funny. Everybody did.

Jimmy offered to bring Skylar home. But home was only down the block. Lisa Marie said she'd walk with her and the girls went off, whispering about us.

They missed the two policemen coming around and clearing out the party. The police said for us to break it up in a way that said to me that they'd been where we were, that they wished they still were. The police asked if there were any adults there. Jake was sweating. Then Jimmy stepped forward, even though he was only seventeen like me. He was the only one in dry clothes by then. The only one who didn't reek of beer. Neither questioned him. Jimmy said he'd make sure the party ended peacefully. The police ambled off and almost everyone else did too.

Only a handful of guys stayed, all good friends, on the football and baseball team with me. The princes of the senior class, my parents would call us, and totally embarrass me. We'd all end up following Jimmy anywhere he wanted to go.

That August night, Jimmy said he wanted us all to do tequila shots together. Everyone was into it. We gathered around him on the deck. He stood. The rest of us sprawled on whatever chairs we could grab. The ever eager Jake supplied a dusty gift bottle of tequila from his parents' liquor cabinet and a dozen even dustier shot glasses. We copied Jimmy, flipping back the shots in unison.

After the second shot, Jimmy wrapped his arm around the back of my chair and said, "Listen. You and me are going to have a great senior year," and I was happy and drunk and it took me a moment to realize that I was relieved too. I agreed wholeheartedly. I listened.

Jake made to pour us all a third shot. He held up the square bottle from Mexico and cheered, "Who's ready for another?" But Jimmy said that all of us had had enough. Remarkably, we listened. Then he said, "I need a ride home." I was chosen. He had to give me a hand to get out of the low-slung chair, my legs and brain no longer working together. Everybody thought that was funny, especially me, or especially the other Sean, the one who vied to be at Jimmy's side, his best friend, his second lieutenant.

I gave him my car keys instead. I only lived down the block. That night I let him take the car without me.

I don't know why things ever went so far. I just don't know, and I can't think. I pull my plaid blanket over my head and cry.

My father bangs through the house. I don't know if he's coming or going to work today. I lost track of his schedule this week. My mother always knew his schedule. She'd always be up to say good-bye to him. Sometimes I'd find her in the backyard, sometimes in that flowered kimono robe that she loved. Dawn full on her bloodless face. She'd be sipping hot tea, having risen with my father at five a.m. "Hope is a thing with feathers," she liked to say, and when I looked confused, she'd add more lines, as if that helped. I haven't been in the backyard since she died.

This morning, Wednesday, I can't get out of bed. I can't face school, I mean, without Jimmy. And it's my birthday.

I flip into the hollow next to me, Jimmy's space. When we slept together, Jimmy could have taken up the whole twin bed eas-ily, but he didn't. He'd lie on his back, near the window. Even in the winter we slept with the window wide open, in case my father came home unexpectedly. He never did. I curled in the crook of his arm, listening to his heart as he talked or slept. He'd nestle me. My head fit exactly into his shoulder blades. I'd run my tongue over his teeth, clean, sharp-tasting of mint, he always brushed be-fore coming over. I'd twine my legs over his jeans. His feet, in white socks, hung off the edge of the bed.

I started paying attention then to my father's schedule. I wanted to know when he was working overnight. I'd tell Jimmy and he'd be there within a half hour of my father pulling out of the driveway.

On those nights, Jimmy was careful to protect me from falling off the edge of the bed. He'd hold fast to me. I'd inhale his scent, warm, full of sweat and fields. I said it was impossible for me to sleep with him so near; he said that he could only sleep with me. Now this twin bed is too big without him.

I can't stop thinking about last night, when he finally called. Collect. I screamed into the phone that I'd accept the charges.

"You're staying strong, Sky?" he asked. He said my name like a country singer, with a twang, with a reaching for the heavens, even though he was born on Long Island like the rest of us. He said my name and I belonged with him.

"Staying strong?" he whispered, more gently the second time. This was what Jimmy had said to me all year instead of *I love you*. I was okay with that. I couldn't expect a guy like Jimmy to just blurt out *I love you*.

He had to say it in his own time, that was Lisa Marie's point.

And Jimmy was something different. He was always so sure of himself and of what the world should be for us. *What the world should be, for us*. That's how he said it, quiet and determined, looking me straight in the eye. Nobody ever questioned him. I didn't, did I?

By the end of last summer Jimmy had made it clear to everyone, shocking me, shocking Lisa Marie more, that he wanted me as his girl. That's how he put it, kind of old-fashioned, that I was Jimmy's girl. Of course, Lisa Marie then became even more crazed to be someone's girl, but it's not like that in our town. Everyone hangs together. Jimmy and I were the odd ones, a couple.

His voice breaks into my thoughts even now, my head stuck under my comforter.

"Are you staying strong?"

That was last night, on the phone. I was afraid to answer. If I started talking, I wouldn't stop, and all I wanted to do was listen to the sound of his voice. Jimmy is my first love; my only. My parents had been that way. Met in high school and stayed together even though I often wondered why, with my mother quoting Emily Dickinson, and my father watching the Mets. All year, I had felt safe in the sound of Jimmy's voice, talking for hours, me gorging myself on words; him, always there. He saved me from going crazy after my mom died.

Last night, his voice was more urgent, more questioning but still deep, drumlike. My heart slammed against my chest, listening.

"Remember that bird, Sky?"

I sobbed for air. How could I ever forget? I smeared the tears away. I fell in love with him beginning with that bird.

"The first night we met?" Jimmy murmured. He could always read my thoughts, my sadness. "You're going to stay strong like that bird?"

I toppled into his voice. I had to restrain myself to only one word. "Yes."

"You're going to stay true?"

"Yes."

"My father told me you're coming to visit me. Are you coming? Is that your birthday present?" he kidded.

"Yes."

"You know I love you, Sky."

Yes. Yes. Yes. That was the first time he said that he loved me. I was stunned. I wanted to hear it again. Say it again. Say it a million times. Each word was distinctive from the previous word: *I—love—you—Sky*. I'd follow this voice everywhere, and then I knew that was the problem; so would others, and he knew it too.

My father bellows for me. I can't get out of bed. Like Lisa Marie always says, I have to focus.

Last night, Jimmy had said, "I love you, Sky," and he waited for me to say it back. I could have blurted it out. *I love you.* But I wanted it to be the most meaningful three words I had ever spoken. I'd never heard "I love you" from anyone but my mother. I wanted to save it to say to him in person. I don't know how I will say it . . . slow . . . fast . . . burst it out . . . maybe pass him a note so he can keep it forever, and I realized then that I'm afraid I won't be able to say it with all the meaning those words deserve. I wish it was all a dream: last weekend, my entire senior year, everything, except for the *I love you*. When I see him, it will be the first thing I say, maybe the only. I drop my face down into the cold space on my bed, wishing I could smell him, remembering the sweat and sharp soap and baby powder, the scratch of blond hair on his cheeks, his powerful arms.

Ever since I heard his voice I've been thinking of one thing. He must have a reason for what happened. I didn't ask on the phone, of course. It was too short a call and I could tell he couldn't really talk. But he had to have a reason. I mean, something more must have happened that night. Something I didn't see in that blur of moon. I couldn't hear everything that was said between Jimmy and that older brother, especially when he first approached the car. I was just that far enough away for some of the talk to sound like flitters or squawks, not words. Maybe he threatened Jimmy. He was a grown man, and Jimmy and Sean were only kids, high school kids like me, throwing out stupid words. They didn't believe what they were saying. They were kids with a bat in the car from baseball practice, not for anything else. They're not guilty. Jimmy's *not* guilty. He's not.

Except as I'm thinking this I'm hearing Lisa Marie's voice in my head. I want to hear it in my own voice. He's. Not. Guilty. I say each word aloud, each syllable separately like a foreign word, to stop Lisa Marie's voice from shackling mine. *Not guilty.* I need to see him. I will, today. *Not guilty.* He'll tell me what to think, I mean, the reason, something I didn't see or hear, something I'm not thinking of because Lisa Marie and my father and everyone else are making me lose my mind. He'll explain it all. He'll be Jimmy. My voice splinters in my head. Instead of *Not guilty,* it practices, *I love you,* three times fast. I know all I have to do is say that, see him, and listen.

I sit up. I have to stay strong and true. I'm barely a hundred pounds. (I quickly convert that into kilos, one of the easiest math team questions last year). How strong can I be?

True and strong. Strong and true. Hope. A thing with feathers. Weight in kilos: 45.4. The smell of bacon, burning, smoking. More banging in the kitchen, my father barks out, "Breakfast," and I rise.

Outside my bedroom, two people jump out at me. I grab for the wall, cover my ears, and duck my head. I have to pee; I'll wet my sweatpants.

"Happy birthday!" shouts Lisa Marie. "I thought I'd make your day."

A few feet beyond Lisa Marie, my dad is standing by the stove. He has egg and grease stains on his EMT uniform. He hasn't shaved. "Happy birthday," he grunts too. "Lookit, Lisa Marie even remembered. She brought a cupcake."

I used to love birthday cupcakes. My mother always made me one, chocolate with chocolate frosting, even the frosting homemade, full of butter. On the countertop, amid the dirty pots and plates, is the one Lisa Marie bought from Towne Bakery, bigger, the icing higher, swirled, dashed with sugar confetti, more perfect than any cupcake my mother ever made, and this makes me sad. I want a lopsided cupcake, with too much icing and a pink candle perched off-center stuck in the top. I want my mother to sing off-key to me.

Instead, Lisa Marie envelops me in the narrow hall. Her hair is bright and fresh-washed. She's wearing a black tank top, a tiny gold cross at her neck, and neon-orange jeans. If she stood on her head, she'd look like a candle.

"Why did you come?"

"I'm always here for your birthday and I always will be." She smooths my hair down, off my face, fills her arms with me. I close my eyes and think of everyone who is not here: Jimmy, my mother. I wrap my arms around her. She hugs me back with all her might.

"Let me go," I finally say, and dash three steps into the bathroom. I can hear Lisa Marie giggling to my father, crashing around the kitchen in her flip-flops. I don't come out until my father, ramming his palm into the door, says, "Did you drown in there? Breakfast is ready. Come see what Lisa Marie did." I pull myself together, splash cold water on my face, wish I could wash away the rings under my eyes, add color to my pale cheeks. I square my shoulders and rummage for the least dirty black T-shirt and jeans in the laundry bin and slip them on. I can do this today.

The smell of bacon and sugar and chocolate and Lisa Marie and my father and me collide in too tight a space. Lisa Marie hasn't been in our house since the day of the funeral. If she's shocked at the mess, she doesn't show it. She is clearing off the square kitchen table, spreading out a paper HAPPY BIRTHDAY tablecloth and matching paper plates. She has a bouquet of balloons tied to my chair.

My father waves his spatula over a fry pan; an egg carton and a loaf of bread clutter the counter. "Who wants eggs? Bacon? Lookit, I even got toast. Whole wheat for you ladies? I wasn't expecting guests, but I got enough for everybody."

I want to say I'm not hungry because I'm not. Except for seeing Jimmy, I wish it wasn't my birthday. I'm not a big birthday person like Lisa Marie. Last year, she had planned a spa day for her and me. I had never been to a spa before, and after some persuasion, I said I'd go. But when my mother took a turn for the worse, I just couldn't leave her side. So Lisa Marie had two chipper spa ladies come here. In the backyard, in side-by-side lawn chairs, a purple iris turban on her bald head, my mother had a manicure and pedicure and a shoulder massage, and so did I. Lisa Marie set out green tea and ginger cookies for us. My mother flashed her nails and wriggled her toes like a kid. That was my real birthday present. My mother died three and a half weeks later, her nails red-hot red.

Lisa Marie squeals in my ear, "Aren't you excited about seeing Jimmy today?"

I hug her again, though my stomach churns. I taste acid in my throat. I want to crawl back into bed. Except I can't. All I want to do is see Jimmy.

"So who's eating?" my father asks, turning to Lisa Marie as if she would save him too.

"I already had breakfast, Mr. Thompson. But I'll have some coffee. Black."

"Good girl. What about you, kiddo?"

"Nothing."

"Lookit. I made your favorite. Scrambled eggs."

"I like my eggs over easy."

"Then I'll make them over easy for you. No problem. I'm easy." He whistles, slamming two eggs down on the side of my mother's black cast-iron fry pan. They crack and spit in the grease. "Doesn't take long. Sit down, girls. I'll serve you."

There's a long white business envelope on my seat. I tear it open. Four crumpled tens and three twenties, one taped. I've never before received money for my birthday.

"Dad?"

My father flips the eggs. "Lookit, I didn't know what to get you. But maybe you and Lisa Marie can go shopping together."

"I'd love to," says Lisa Marie, pouring coffee into a paper cup since there aren't any clean mugs. "We could go today after school."

"I can't."

"Why not?" says my father, serving me up two eggs slick with bacon grease. "Need salt with that?"

"I'm going to visit Jimmy."

"No, you're not." He slams open a cabinet. "Where do we keep the salt?"

"Yes. I'm eighteen. I can go visit by myself."

"You're not going in that, are you?" says Lisa Marie, bumping into the balloons as my father squeezes by her.

I sniff down at my T-shirt. Maybe I can find another to wear. I look straight at him. "I'm going to visit Jimmy today."

"You're not missing school," he sputters.

"I'm going. I'll go after last period, if that makes you happy."

"You're not going to visit anyone in jail." Another cabinet flies open and closed. Most of them are half empty. "Especially on your birthday."

"It is Jimmy, Mr. Thompson." Lisa Marie comes to my defense, and I want to run to her side, but my father pushes between us.

"I don't care if it's the president." He tackles open almost every cabinet, working his way around the kitchen, even flinging open the cabinet where my mother kept her vitamins and medicines and syringes, now completely empty. I shudder. He knows what was in there too and backs away.

"I don't need salt, Dad," I shout. "I'm not eating these eggs."

"You're eating."

"I'm going to see Jimmy. That's all I want for my birthday. I want to see Jimmy—"

"Here's the damn salt. Sit down and eat."

"Maybe I can help?" offers Lisa Marie, stepping between us, taking the saltshaker from his hands, and placing it on the table.

"Lookit. This is between me and my daughter. I appreciate you coming over this morning. But I don't want my daughter involved with Jimmy Seeger no more. Not after last Saturday night. Not after seeing what she's seen."

"You told your father you were there?" Lisa Marie hisses. "I can't believe you. What have we been talking about? Focus, Skylar. Focus."

"He's the only one. But I didn't tell him any details." I turn and face him. "Don't worry. He didn't want to know any details. He doesn't like the truth."

"That's an interesting thing to say about your father," adds Lisa Marie in her psychologist-in-training voice.

"What the hell does that mean? Lookit, what truth? Tell me." He addresses this to Lisa Marie and not to me.

She shrugs. "Don't look at me. I know nothing. I have to get going. I'll see you in school, Skylar. Remember: Everybody knows. Nobody's talking."

"What's that?" asks my father, raising his head off his chest.

"Just a fun end-of-year thing, Mr. Thompson." Lisa Marie whirls me into another hug. "I'm so excited you're seeing Jimmy, aren't you?" she whispers, and hurries out the door.

My father fumbles his big hand across his gray stubble. "Lookit, Skylar. It's your birthday. I want you to have a happy one."

How is that ever going to happen?

"Let's talk. We haven't talked since I don't know when. Never."

I slide past him and slam shut the cabinets one by one until I come to my mother's space. I search in there as if I expect to find something. Not even a single pill. He cleaned out every shelf.

"You want to tell me what happened last Saturday night? If

you think it will help you, tell me. I'm all ears." He turns his back on me, scraping burned ends of eggs and bacon on top of the dishes piled in the sink.

I ease close that last cabinet. "I'm taking Jimmy's side," I say. "I'm not having another person leave me because I said too much."

"What are you talking about, Skylar? Maybe you do need to go back to the school psychologist. Or someone private? You can use your birthday money for that," he says, as if there were something funny in all this. "Lookit, I'm only kidding. We can afford someone for you to talk with—"

"You're an EMT," I cut in, my heart drumming against my ribs. "You see people die all the time. She said she asked you."

"Asked me what?" He doesn't stop working on the fry pan, scraping it, making a bigger mess in the sink, on the floor.

"She said."

"What?"

"She said that she asked you if it was okay to die. And, you said no."

Now he stops. The spatula clatters off into the sink. The fry pan looks scarred.

I push my way over to him. I don't need to shout this across birthday balloons. "So she asked me. To tell her the truth."

"She had stopped the chemo treatments—but I thought there was something else, maybe something experimental—"

"What mother asks her daughter if it's okay to die?" I say. "And what daughter says yes?"

"Skylar, let me just finish with this and we can talk. Lookit, we can go somewhere, away from here, talk."

"My mother asked. And I said it was okay to die. Someday. I

said that while she was curled like a little girl on your bed in pain and I was at her side, holding both her hands in my own. I told her the truth, and what did it get me? She died that night. So much for the truth. You should have been there." I look at him, wishing he were dead and not her.

"I had to work. Your mother understood that." He wipes his hands on his pants legs. "Let's sit together and eat something. Please."

I pick up Lisa Marie's perfect chocolate birthday cupcake and mash it in my mouth. "I'm done here."

Principal

Bell rings. First period. Some nights I hear school bells in my sleep. I shoot right up. My husband doesn't even wake up anymore when I do this. I have to remember—two more years until retirement. On my first trip after I retire, I plan to tango in Buenos Aires, hike up to Machu Picchu, go far away from here—far from these halls and maybe even far from my husband. I haven't decided on that yet. I need someone with an adventuresome spirit for the next stage of my life. Recently, I feel like I've been on an adventure that has gone off the path.

I acknowledge Jake Kroll, the shortest student in school. I'm rewarded with a mumbled, "Morning." If that was James Seeger, he would have grinned like he owned the place, and I would have grinned back. Beyond his athletic success, he cochaired the annual school Blood Drive, our most successful ever, with Lisa Marie Murano. I am expecting a certificate from the Red Cross to present to him at graduation.

I do not know if he will be present at graduation or not. I assume he will not be. All my attention now needs to be on protecting the school's image, and the students' privacy, of course.

This is basically a good school.

Officially, we score in the top quartile of schools in the county, sometimes in the top half, depending upon which jurisdiction and which test our kids are taking. We've become a testing culture. Everything is measured. That's the biggest difference I've seen over the years. We gear everyone up for the test. We offer special breakfasts like the kids are on a marathon. We've had relaxation specialists, aka the superintendent's wife who teaches yoga, in for the kids and the teachers. We pull out the low performers and pound them with basic facts. Some of the testing has been positive, don't get me wrong. I go along with the program that we need to know how our kids are performing academically. But everything in life cannot be boiled down to a number. And not everything in life can or should be taught at school.

Our school population is overwhelmingly white. Some Asians, or more precisely East Asians, Indians from India or Bengalis, I'm not sure what they are called, I should research it, from Bangladesh. One very nice Bangladesh family runs the local Dunkin' Donuts. Those kids bring up the test scores. In recent years, some Hispanics have moved in on the fringes. They rent the smaller houses along the railroad tracks or illegal apartments in some houses. Our taxes are high even for Long Island and our people are trying to hold on to their houses, especially older people, so they set up apartments in basements or garages. Our town strongly discourages this based on quality-of-life issues and it has been kept to a minimum, unlike in other places on the island.

To be clear, we're not the north shore of the island, the Gold Coast, the truly high-spending school districts. Our district isn't wealthy by Long Island standards, or poor. I always say we're comfortably in the middle. The town next door, where those two brothers live, reportedly with their aunt and uncle, is an entirely different case. The population statistics are reversed. The poverty rate is high. Then again, social services are offered for their benefit. That is our island. Each town wants to be its own island.

At our high school, we are very proud that our school has

excelled in athletics and academics. This spring, we were one of the top schools in the number of Scholar-Athletes, students who outperformed both in the letter of their sports and grade-point average.

The photo of all our Scholar-Athletes with the school superintendent and the school board made front-page news in the weekly neighborhood newspaper. Unfortunately, Coach Martinez was cut out of that picture, but it was an oversight. The school board, a group that I will not go on the record as either praising or damning, for I have outlived many a school board and am two years away from receiving my pension, recognized Coach Martinez at the last meeting.

Mrs. Mayer, the head of the school board, felt compelled to speak in Spanish to the coach. I cringed at her poor Spanish. Everyone could see how embarrassed the man was in her overperfumed presence. He was not the kind who liked being fawned over by overweight PTA mothers. She practically threatened the school if Coach Martinez did not give her son, Sean, a recommendation. Didn't she object to the hiring of Coach Martinez on the basis of his lack of administrative experience? And now she wants his recommendation for her son.

Our office keeps bracing itself for the Mayers or Seegers to storm in. Blame the professional staff, or even Coach Martinez, who has remained very professional, going about his business teaching, coaching varsity baseball. But we must remain very clear about our position. This incident happened off school grounds. If there were rumors about what was going on in the school, no one was officially made aware of them.

I quicken my step, lock my office door behind me, and steal

another look at the photo on my wall of fame. Yes. Both of them. Jimmy Seeger and Sean Mayer are in that front-page picture standing shoulder to shoulder. Jimmy isn't smiling. I had never noticed that before now.

This fall he was new to our district. You couldn't help but notice him. Jimmy was taller than most of the teachers, wore his hair in a military crew cut. He was planning to join the Army, or was it the Marines? One noticed Jimmy. He was a natural leader. I will admit that he and Coach Martinez had a personality clash. But I like my teachers, especially the coaches, to understand that it is their job to keep discipline in the classrooms or on the field.

In this case, however, Coach Martinez requested a meeting with Jimmy's parents for which I was present. We gathered in my office last fall, the week before the big Thanksgiving game: Jimmy and his father. His mother was working. Mr. Seeger, who was as tall as Jimmy, walked with a cane. He had a full thick head of white hair and I could see where Jimmy inherited his penetrating blue eyes.

Mr. Seeger had been injured on 9/11. A first responder, is what someone told me. As we sat in my office, I should have noticed that Jimmy's father was looking only at me. Now, this is only my opinion. But Mr. Seeger had these eyes that didn't blink, that were fixed on my own. I thought it was out of respect for my position as the high school principal, but I have since come to the conclusion that it was a lack of respect for both me and Coach Martinez. Now, this is only my opinion. But in that meeting, last November, in my office, he accused Coach Martinez of singling out his son, giving him extra laps and push-ups during football practice. He went roughly on offense. He was loud and uncouth, but no more so than a lot of hotheaded parents who feel like they and their kids are entitled to more. He threatened that he would pull Jimmy out of the Turkey Bowl. No one wanted that to happen, not even Coach Martinez. Mr. Seeger said all this fixed on me, without once looking, not even once, in my opinion, at Coach Martinez directly.

We went on to lose the Turkey Bowl. But never mind.

I slip the framed photo off my wall. Even without a smile, Jimmy is handsome and confident; Sean Mayer is slouching and grinning. To be perfectly honest, Sean Mayer would never be in this picture without Jimmy Seeger being an example to him, and to a lot of our young athletes, about the value of working hard academically. Sean Mayer has made bail. I've heard the Seeger family is having trouble. Both boys are stars of the baseball team. Do I permit Sean, or Jimmy, for that matter, if he is released, to play the last game of the baseball season on Sunday? I must discuss this with the superintendent.

We may be a middle-class community teetering on the edge of something, but I'm not sure what that is and certainly won't make any pronouncements that are outside my role as an educator.

No press is allowed inside the building or to talk to the students anywhere on school property without written permission of their parents. I have informed our very able security guard of this policy. I have also strongly suggested that none of our teachers express any public opinions on this matter. None have, to my knowledge.

I will concede that there was some particular undercurrent in the school this spring. But this is by no means a school issue. If the police are finding these young people and their parents reluctant to participate in their investigation, then it is an issue between the police and the students and their parents. This unfortunate incident happened after school hours, off school property.

I glance down at my cluttered desk. On top of all the end-of-year forms, grade reviews, graduation procedural memos, is a note. Mr. Lake, the Advanced Placement math teacher, would like to meet with me regarding Skylar Thompson. The note is on a pink message slip in my secretary's ancient Catholic school script handwriting, which has grown more spidery and indecipherable over the past twenty-three years. She checked the urgent box. I have no intentions of rushing to speak with him about Skylar Thompson.

A smart girl like that should have confided in an adult if indeed what people say was going on was going on. No student said anything to any adult in an official capacity about "beaner-hopping." I thought it sounded like a dance. *Never mind.* I slide the framed newsprint photo forcibly into my desk. No use advertising the Scholar-Athletes at this point in the school year.

Though I do think that we will come to understand that there was something else behind this particular incident. Perhaps the two boys were provoked in some way. I just cannot believe that boys that go to my school, two Scholar-Athletes, about to graduate, would act in such a way. Like I keep saying, this is a good school. But never mind.

The school quiets, the settling in after the bell rings. I pull out a brochure for summer volunteer vacations. I am thinking of switching my summer plans. Instead of a cruise to Alaska, perhaps I will take this summer to join others helping indigent populations in Central America. Though, truthfully, I don't want to go somewhere too hot. These last three days, in fact this entire year, have tested me.

Gloria Cortez

Mother of Arturo and Carlos Cortez

Translated from Spanish

Arturo is in the critical care. I know he will be okay. God willing. He is strong. He will recover from this beating.

I am waiting for a special visa to permit me back into the United States. I am at the airport in the capital, in San Salvador, waiting for the American authorities. They have asked me to stay in this office where there are no windows, only a desk and a hard-backed chair, and I am alone.

I should never have come back to El Salvador. But my own mother was dying. I was her only daughter. My brother sent me back. He said I must, and so I did. I left my oldest son, Arturo, seven years old, with him and his wife. They had no children of their own. My brother is very respectable. He has been in the United States long enough to benefit from a special amnesty, I think this was in 1986. Everybody who could became a citizen. Yet I returned. Yes, to El Salvador, to one room with no running water, to care for my ailing mother.

I did bring with me Carlos. He was born in America, that is the truth. He was an infant when I brought him with me to El Salvador. And my brother sent money, thank God, enough for us to live, for me to fix my mother's house, add two rooms, a proper roof, and indoor plumbing.

I thought I would find a way back to Long Island someday. But after my mother died, my aunt was sick, then my uncle, and others.

All the old ones were dying and I was the only one here to care for them. To bury them.

When it was time for Carlos to go to grade school, I sent him to America alone. He joined Arturo in Long Island at the home of my brother and his wife. That was eleven years ago. These days, my sons beg me to file papers, to interview, for the visa. I promise them that I am working on it. These things take time.

Arturo even said he would find out about other ways. He would pay the man you have to pay, we don't even call them men, but animals, coyotes, to get me over the border. I am too old to go that route again, I say to him.

I have seen pictures of my brother's house. Such a nice house. The back of the house is along the railroad tracks, but nobody minds the trains, they tell me. The house is painted white with blue shutters like the colors of the flag of El Salvador. There is a green yard dotted with daffodils, yellow flowers like happy children. My brother even put in a new white fence this year. Both Carlos and Arturo helped.

Yes, yes, Arturo went to school. But he was more of a worker than a schoolboy. At sixteen, he left school, and my brother, a good man, taught him his trade, masonry. My brother gives me very good reports. He said that the big boss called Arturo "meticulous" in his work. I liked this word so much I rolled it on my tongue for days afterward.

But I have not seen them in all these years, my sons. Eleven years. I always thought that when we were reunited there would be only joy in our hearts. They have grown to be men without me.

The one thing they keep with them, from me, is my last name.

The truth be told, Arturo once asked me if we had Spanish blood in us because of our name: Cortez. It is the name of a famous conquistador. My own father always liked to tell me we had Spanish blood in us. My father wanted a better life for us too. And what happened? The army killed him during the civil wars here. The soldiers stormed our village and murdered all the men, a dozen old farmers, in the fields when nobody would take up with them. My father was hacked to death by a machete in the bean fields. That is the truth.

I thought my father was an old man. I am older now than he was at his death. I am forty-two years of age. You would think that I left my country when I was young because of such violence. No, no, I left to follow a man. Yes, I found him and he gave me Carlos and left me.

When Arturo asked about our Spanish blood, I said the same thing my father had told me. I wanted him to be proud and strong. But we do not look like we have much Spanish blood in us. We are too dark. Or, as Arturo joked, once he sensed I had stretched the truth, "We are permanently tanned. *Mamí,* people spend a lot of money in tanning salons here to look like us." He likes to tease me on our weekly phone calls.

Arturo never said anything bad or mean about nobody. He would never have started anything up with those boys. He has never been arrested, never caused anyone trouble, never looked for trouble. He has wired me money every month. I have never had to ask.

The last call I had with him, yes, it was last Saturday night, he was meeting Carlos. The two brothers, my sons, were going to a *quinceañera.* "A lot of girls are going to be there, *Mamí.*" He kidded me because he knew I worried about him living in the United States without any papers.

I had urged him to find an American girl to marry him. When I was on Long Island cleaning office buildings, at the beginning of my shift, eight o'clock at night, I would even see a few still at their desks, with nowhere else to go.

"Talk with your uncle about finding one of these girls for you," I had said. Though I had already spoken with my brother about this idea of arranging a marriage for Arturo.

"Maybe find a fat one," I said to Arturo. This is the truth. "A fat American girl, one with a big behind, who would like the attentions of a handsome man like you. You tell her that you love her hair, her eyes. Maybe she's fat and old—thirty years old, maybe, or even older. She will want you. Maybe she will ask you to marry her." My grown-up son laughed at me and said he still hoped to marry for love, someone like me.

But I know something at age forty-two about the loneliness of women. "A little lie, Arturo. So what? And not anyone like me. Someone who went to school. Someone who can do more than mop floors or take care of old people. Someone lucky. Not me." When I was in one of these moods, he could only say that he loved me, and so he did. We both knew—if Arturo could marry, he would become a citizen of the United States of America. His future would be secure. When I see him, I will talk to him about this again.

One minute, please. From somewhere I smell coffee and part of me wants nothing more than a cup of very hot coffee with fresh cream. But I am afraid to go ask anyone for coffee. I have been told by authorities to sit and wait. I feel like I have been waiting my whole life to see my sons again. Sometimes I feel that I am only half here, listening for steps, half in thoughts and half in dreams, and now dreaming of coffee.

When he was age six, I sent Carlos to Arturo. He could not stay with me. He had to learn English. He had to have his chance; he was American-born. I wanted Carlos to go to school in America. And Carlos had what we all desired: an American passport. He was born in Long Island, New York. I had his papers, a birth certificate, his own passport. I kept them next to my heart until I gave them to him like a gift. My brother had paid for Carlos's one-way flight. He always tells me that my sons are inseparable.

It was Carlos who called me from the hospital. He was screaming in English, forgetting his Spanish. My brother had to take the phone from him. I had to hear the news that my sons had been beat up by a gang of white teenagers in Spanish to understand what had happened. Now all I want to do is hold both my sons and never let them go.

A nurse from the hospital telephoned me yesterday, or was it the day before? No, it was yesterday, Tuesday, I spoke with her. I had just eaten a mango, my first food in two days. She was from Colombia and spoke Spanish, but I could not understand her accent very well. My brother translated. All she was telling me was the same thing: there had been no change in Arturo's condition. He has injuries of the head. Yes, head injuries, my son. He is on a ventilator.

After she called, I became a crazy woman. My sons' names roared in my head until I could not talk anymore. I tore at my hair. Gave up my dinner on the floor. I flew into the courtyard like a witch. The neighbors had to carry me to my bed and tie me to the bedposts or I would have injured myself.

The United States police found me too. Under these conditions, they said this to me, yes, an Officer Healey, the United States of America, was expediting a visa. That is the exact word, *expediting.*

Office Healey was very nice, very respectful. I told him that my brother would arrange for a plane ticket. I was not asking for charity. I traveled two hours at dawn to be here for this special visa and have been waiting. Permit me to check my cell phone for the time, for calls. Ah, the phone, it is dead. Yes, I have packed the battery charger Arturo sent me in my bags, but my bags are elsewhere, already checked in.

Yes, today I have pulled back my thick wavy hair into a very nice bun. I wear a dark blue dress borrowed from my mother's closet, the dress of a dead woman, to see my sons. My mother's wedding band is on my finger. When the authorities arrive with the visa, they will see a respectable woman, a mother.

But what if they never come for me? Visas from this country to the United States are denied all the time. Please tell me this will not be so. I must go to my sons. I say this with my hand raised to my heart. I am holding it from breaking.

How many two-by-two-by-two cubes must be added to an eight-by-eight-by-eight cube to make a ten-by-ten-by-ten cube?

That was last year's final question in the Mathlete championship. I'm thinking about this as I drive to the county jail, trying to stay sane. I thought the jail would be a trip somewhere far, isolated, a cove. Yet Google Maps had estimated travel time at eleven minutes from my house.

School was a fog. Bells rang. Only Benny during calculus asked something that was not about Jimmy. Would I come to the Mathlete finals? "As a spectator? We've been drilling for three hours a day, even weekends, for the past month. We're quite prepared. Quite."

Of course I said no. I wished him luck. He reminded me of last year's tournament.

Sixty-one cubes. That was the solution. Easily solved. I had the winning answer. Quite right, as Benny would say.

Now I study the traffic signs. Every left-hand turn is illegal. No U-turns on the turnpike. A two-ton truck and an SUV block my Mustang in. Even if I wanted to make an illegal move, I can't—it'd be difficult—I could get killed.

Finally, a turnaround to the side street where the jail supposedly is located. And the jail? There is no jail. I expected a big sign: county jail this way. Instead, houses that look like my house line up and down the block. Neat boxes on neat lawns. I drive past a high school spread out over the next block, it looks like my high school, except it isn't or I have entered an alternative reality. Then there's a Little League baseball field with players in black-and-white uniforms, a church and a synagogue keeping guard on opposite corners, but no jail. I trail along a fence with green grass and a parking lot, a different no-man's-land, well kept. That's when I peer up out of the top of my windshield and see the barbed wire. Three rows of wire wound like ribbon on top of a steel fence. A modest rectangular sign reads: COUNTY SHERIFF: DEPARTMENT OF CORRECTIONS. I almost miss the entrance.

A two-story black-stone building lies low down the slope of a hill, the first floor more in the ground than above it, serving to obscure it from the street or make you think that it's anything else but a jail. I stare up. Guard towers, higher than the black building, are positioned on each corner. Between each tower is another fence, clearly marked: DANGER, HIGH VOLTAGE. And I know I am here, at a jail. Jimmy's jail. Roars cross the parking lot. I'm startled to hear Little Leaguers cheering. Someone must have hit a home run.

I circle the parking lot, smaller than our school's senior lot, but jammed tighter. I circle again.

NO PICKING UP OR DROPPING OFF ANYONE AT ANY TIME.

NO VISITORS ALLOWED AT OR NEAR THE FENCE.

ALL VISITORS MUST CHECK IN. ALL BAGS SEARCHED. NO EXCEPTIONS.

VISITANTES, with an arrow pointing right.

THE COUNTY SHERIFF OFFICE SUPPORTS THE MEN AND WOMEN STATIONED AROUND THE WORLD IN THE ARMED SERVICES—ESPECIALLY THOSE SERVING IN IRAQ AND AFGHANISTAN.

All these signs are tacked to a pegboard nailed to the front of a red one-room guardhouse at the far end of the parking lot. I'm hoping I can find some help there on where to park or even where the front entrance is. The guard, in his twenties, lean, wiry, approaches me. He sticks his nose, bent like it was broken more than once, at the edge of my open car window.

"Help you?" he says, in razor-sharp shorthand.

I swallow. I can't do this. I can't say I'm here to see my boyfriend. I'm here to see Jimmy. He can't be here. If I go home, maybe he'll be there, just like always. It will be last week or Saturday morning. We'll make plans to go to a movie. It won't be today.

"Where do I park? I mean to visit someone?"

His head shakes back and forth in a deliberately slow rebuke. "Visiting hours. Almost over."

"But if I have to see someone, where do I park?"

"All filled. Try the street. But not out there." He points to the ordinary street running alongside the jail. "We tow cars there."

The tension runs out of me like I have suffered a terrible defeat.

"Back up, miss. Turn around the car. Nice car." He pats the roof of my car, dismissing me.

I don't move. I can't. *I'm here, Jimmy. I'm here,* I want to shout.

"Try Saturday, Miss."

"Saturday?"

"*A* through *M* visit nine a.m. until twelve noon. *M* through *Z* visits twelve noon to three p.m. Got that?"

I stare up at the county jail. "Oh." Jimmy Seeger is a prisoner. *S* equals his last initial; *S* equals afternoon.

"Come early. Parking fills up fast. Not too hard?"

"Not too hard," I repeat, closing my eyes against this heartbreakingly unsolvable world.

Carlos Cortez
Arturo's brother

I am not here.

I am not in the middle of the turnpike. But I am.

I should be at the bus stop, waiting for the bus, going home at this time of night. But I'm not.

I should be at Arturo's side.

But there will be a pile of bills to pay after this is over. So I keep going to work. He'd want me to keep my job. Then, bro, I'll go back to school. I promise.

I squeeze my eyes shut. *I am with Arturo. It's last Saturday night. We're going to the birthday party. I don't know her. Arturo does. He knows everybody. His buddies call him "El Jefe"—the Boss—because he's always making the plans. He's going to own his own masonry company. His plans for me are different.*

"You're too skinny and bony to be a decent mason. You're no good with a trowel or chisel. I'm scared to give you a hammer. No one wants to buy a wall that falls down," he kids me in Spanish. I respond in English that at least I'm not ugly like him. I like his idea about me being a teacher, though I argue with him that we should go into business together. He wants me to go to college. He's the boss.

I waver on the divide. The opposite side, the other bus stop, is there. My legs and arms are sore, bruised. I swear I will hurt those that hurt my brother.

Saturday night, Arturo met me at the restaurant where I bus tables. He brought a present for me, which he pulled out of his scuffed-up gym bag with a flourish: a new shirt. He had one too. They were both in fine silk. Mine was the color of cream; his an electric blue. With his penknife, a slim blade three or four inches long, hardly anything, used to dig the muck out of his nails usually, he carefully cut open my new shirt from its plastic package. He thumbed the penknife back into the center of its fake wood handle, slipped it back into his pants pocket.

He shook the shirt out. The sleeves shimmered, catching the streetlight like a flame. He peeled off his plaid work shirt, folded it into the gym bag, and slid his arms, one then the other, into the sleeves, enjoying the rare feeling of the new on his skin. He's built square, low to the ground, his arms powerful, as if made to be a mason. His silk shirt ran tight across his chest and he had showered and slicked back his hair. Arturo looked ready to dance, to meet girls, to have a very good time.

My shirt was loose and short on my long arms. I looked like nothing, like a kid, next to Arturo. I argued with him that I couldn't go to any party. I stank. I reeked of dishwater. He told me that I was like an old woman, always complaining, never wanting to go anywhere. He threw his arms around my shoulders. "Tuck your shirt in. Act like a man and you'll look like one. Tonight, you're with me and we're going."

Now I stagger down the turnpike's littered concrete divide. Cars pound on their horns. They must think I'm drunk. I almost wish I was. Thoughts fly at me. Should I still go to that GED course at the library next week? I should never have left school, but it was easier than staying in. The library is another matter. I go in with my library card and am treated with respect. Arturo always thought that I was obsessed with the librarians, that I liked how they all treated me like I was a little bit helpless, like a little boy. But he encouraged me to go there. He'd kid me, call me "professor," not without some pride in his voice. He never wanted me to drop out of school. He was always saying I was lucky. Born here. American. Yet he'd know how to find real justice. He'd know the men to talk to. I know nothing.

That night, Arturo marched up and down the side of the road. This very road in El Salvador would be a major highway. Here it's only a road with a grander old name, a turnpike. "Tonight is Saturday night, bro. It's true, the workingman has something to celebrate tonight."

If we were heading home, we'd go the other way. We'd have walked from the restaurant in forty or fifty minutes and been inside the bedroom we shared in the basement of our uncle's house. But I wasn't going to persuade Arturo. The Boss. El Jefe. He wanted a cold beer and a girl and music to dance to and he wanted it in that order.

"I should have borrowed a car," he said for the tenth time when no bus showed up. He yawned. He had been at work since seven o'clock in the morning. He rose with the sun. He always said each day starts new.

It was a dry, clear, full-moon spring night. New buds, grasses, a faint smell of sea salt drifted in the air. And, in my new shirt, I was starting to get excited at the idea that maybe I could meet a girl. At school, I had kept to myself. I never fit in anywhere, even when I played baseball. I was a decent second baseman, but I didn't have the right temperament, according to my coach. I wasn't good enough. Stroking that new shirt, that beautiful new shirt, I felt more confident than usual.

Even though he was tired, Arturo was full of good spirits. He had a reason to be full of hope. He had found his way to a new Social Security number. He slid it out of his wallet, cupped it in his hand. He even had the official identification card to go with it. He studied it. "I wish I didn't have to buy it. Or pay so much to buy it. I wish it was easier to get my papers. And be like you. A citizen of the United States of America. But with these numbers, I will do well by your country, bro." He whistled a few bars of "God Bless America" and kissed the card.

"Maybe we should hitchhike to the party?" I suggested. "We don't want to get there too late."

Arturo didn't like that idea. We were on the border of our town. Cops were always patrolling in our neighborhood, but I didn't see any here. I didn't like the dark at all. This borderland has dollar stores, check cashing, cheap nameless fried chicken, and a few chain restaurants like the one I work at. No signs announce the border, but everything changes just past it: the people, the cars, the schools. No one hitchhikes from here to there, but I thought that hitchhiking would be an easy fix. Someone we knew, someone like us, would pick us up. Arturo paced.

The fact that the party was in the town next door was a big deal. Arturo said that the girl's family was from Ecuador. Her father was a contractor, and he had done very well. He had moved up. He had bought and rented out houses in our neighborhood. I remember thinking that Arturo wanted to meet the father as much as dance with the daughter. That was cool. He was always thinking, my brother.

Arturo craned his neck up and down the four-lane turnpike to see if there was a cop anywhere to hassle us. He was always cautious like that.

"I have something too," I said, grinning.

"What do you have, bro?"

I shook two baggies of weed out of my backpack.

"Shit."

"Supposed to be good," I said.

"Good? Good?"

This wasn't good. I stepped back. Behind me was a field, a vacant lot, in front of me traffic.

"Her whole family will be there. If they see us with this, I won't ever be given a job."

I had an answer for that. "It's not for the party. I heard that these are an easy sell at the train station in that town. That's what Angie, from the restaurant, said to me. We can catch a cab back home then."

He grabbed the bags from me. "What are you? Stupid?" He stuffed the weed into his gym bag. "I'm holding on to this. Nobody is acting stupid tonight. You think you would have learned something from me. Like how not to be stupid."

I lurched out into the empty pavement. I was going to get us a ride. I wanted to be with other people who treated me with respect, unlike Arturo, who thought I was still a child.

He laughed, put his arm tight around me. "It's true. You have no luck. But stay with me. I do."

Cars race by now on the turnpike as they did then. I am balanced on the sliver of the divide. I could get killed. Death would be easy, easier than this.

Nobody would stop for us. How many minutes passed? The moon rose full, yearning for us, in the sky. Arturo suggested lightly, "It's late. No buses running, not too many cars even, and nobody willing to stop for two ugly dudes like us. This is going to be a story for you to tell Mom." He strode back and forth as if willing the bus to arrive. "When was the last time you spoke with her?"

It had been several days. Maybe a week even. I shrugged.

"I talk to her every day," said Arturo, pacing in front of that damned bus stop.

"I have nothing to say to her."

"You just don't want her to know that you dropped out of high school."

"Like you."

He punched my shoulder, harder than either of us expected. His fists were like rock, like the stone he worked with every day. He made kissing sounds at my arm, which made it hurt more.

(It would take two of them, one with a baseball bat, to beat Arturo down.)

"Don't you miss anything about school?" Arturo asked, all casual-like.

"Nah," I replied, wanting him to back away, give me space, but he didn't. "Last time I talked to her she told me she missed her interview at the embassy again. She isn't even trying to get back here—" My voice cracked. The last thing Arturo would stand for was me not respecting our mother. "When was the last time you saw her? Eleven years ago. She just wants to live off the money you send her—"

"You want me to tear that shirt from your back, Carlito?"

I should have said something else. Got him to fight me. Beat me to a pulp. We'd have gone back to our rooms, with our beds across from one another, pissed off, mad, alive. Cars whiz by. I feel like I am balancing on a cliff.

"I'm going now," I said, walking away from him and sticking my thumb back out. I'd get to the party by myself, and if I did, I'd maybe meet the girl who'd change my life, the one who'd show me how to dance the merengue as effortlessly as Arturo or anyone. She'd understand why I wasn't in school and why I wanted to go back. She'd kiss me. She'd speak perfect English and Spanish. My mother would love her.

"Carlito," said Arturo, following me, launching into one of his speeches, "I started this day with the sun. I built an entire walkway and front steps. The brick swayed around a tree. My work made this plain old house look like a mansion. All you did was wash a few dishes. I am tired to the inside of my bones, bro. Next time I'll borrow a car to drive to the party in style. Even so, put that thumb in your pocket and let's start walking to that party."

I should have walked with you those four or five miles. Back to our room. I should have carried you on my back. "Arturo!"

He dug his knuckles into my cheek. He flung his arm over my shoulders, hugging me to his side. I was happy. We were heading off, together. I even said that I would call our mother the next day. He liked that. And then a sleek black SUV skidded to a stop a few yards from us, off the turnpike, in the shadows of that vacant lot. The voices in the car shouted, "Where're you heading?"

I tossed back to them the name of the town just down the turnpike. "You really going there, man?" shouted the voice. There was laughing. They were high school kids. I didn't recognize them. But I knew them. The guys with cars and girls. And I wanted to go to this party so bad and meet my girl. "Arturo, let's go, man. We have a ride!"

He hesitated. He was smarter than me. "Let me go over there, bro, and check them out." They were shouting something more at us. A tractor-trailer rattled by. We couldn't hear them.

My brother unwove his arm from around my shoulder. He cuffed my head. He wanted to go to the party too. We thought we were lucky. We had a ride. We didn't see the baseball bat, or I didn't—until it was too late. And then we heard, "Beaners. Stupid. Mexicans. Go. Home. Let's go. Let's go. Get them. Let's go," words I will never forget.

Exhaust from another truck engulfs me. The ground swirls. Or, maybe I'm dead too. I am with you, Arturo. You cannot be dead when I am alive. I crumble down to my knees on the narrow divide.

Take me instead.

I have avoided this place.

This square plot of land. The lawn chairs, abandoned outside all winter, flung on their metal sides. The hoe and rake fallen to the ground. The flowerbed, choked with leaves. Twigs caught in the rosebushes, winter's debris—

My mother loved flowers. Even at the end, she leaned upon me, more bones than skin, and I lowered her to the ground, to prune, to weed, to turn the earth between our fingers, among her roses. She'd sneak a cigarette and make me swear not to tell my father. She had quit. Before I was born.

I haven't taken care of her roses. American Beauties. I haven't watered or mulched or pruned. I haven't done anything I said I'd do.

The lights from other houses warned me off. The smell of dinners kept me inside. That and Jimmy, of course.

When we weren't together, he'd called me—how many times a day? He always wanted to know where I was, what I was thinking.

I went along with whatever he said. Meet at eight after practice. Meet at midnight because we hadn't seen each other in four hours. Or once, even, meet at three a.m. and go watch the sun rise on the beach in Montauk, just the two of us.

He had something he always said. *There are two places in life, first place and no place*. I mean, I think that's what he always said. I should have listened harder. But he said that, about winners and losers, us and them, to all of us, not just me. And somehow that translated into beaner-hopping. Find them, chase them, knock them to the ground, and run. We win. Everyone wanted to be part of it. We didn't think it would go so far. I'm sure Jimmy didn't. If Jimmy had known that this would be the future, he'd have driven somewhere else that night, maybe out to Montauk, out to the beach, to the sand in our hair and our kisses. If I had known, I would have said something to Jimmy, wouldn't I have?

I need to see him. Saturday. The thing is, I have to call his house and I haven't done that yet. I'm going to do that now. Right now. The rosebushes bend, their leaves are mottled, speckled in the moonlight, limp to my touch. My mother loved mud-splattered knees, hands full of earth, blooming plants.

On Saturday, I'll be the first one on line. I'm not going to say anything to anybody but him. It'll be okay then. Jimmy will get out. We'll have the greatest summer of our lives. We'll go out east to Montauk, to the lighthouse, to the end, to fish, to drink beer on the beach, to follow the sun rising over the water, to the end.

"Or the beginning?" I once joked with Jimmy. "Maybe Montauk is where it all begins?"

He insisted it was the end. That's the way he saw things. There was a right way and a wrong way, a beginning and an end. All the bumper stickers said MONTAUK, THE END.

I have to buy fertilizer. Wasn't that on the list my mother left me? Or was it spray? I have to buy bug spray for the roses? Or food? She wanted me to feed her roses. They must be starving. The bushes rustle. I have to go. I have to get out of this backyard, away from her rosebushes without blooms, out of her yard. I want to focus only on Jimmy—

"Sky-lar. Sky-laaar!"

The call crosses the hedge. A trace of roast beef spirals toward me. My eyes narrow against the invasion of light. I'm exhausted, hungry, and pivoting toward my dark house. I don't want to be with anybody.

"Skylar!"

Sean.

"Hey. What's up?"

I tumble through the bushes. I never knew why my mother planted them. I think she didn't want Skylar and me running between our houses like her house was mine and mine hers.

"Skylar," I say, and see her going back into her house. "Hey, Skylar. It's me, Sean." I know this sounds stupid. She knows it's me, not some rapist or murderer. I mean, me, Sean, the Sean that's known her all her life. Not that other Sean. He thought Jimmy was the center of the world. When he found out Jimmy thought the world was flat, that guy believed: sure the world could be flat, why not? And he followed Jimmy off the end.

"Skylar!"

She keeps walking. Until eighth grade or so we were the same height, then in one summer I was twice the size of her. She's slight like her mother was. She shakes her head. Her hair is a mess around her pale face and it flies around her shoulders. It's chilly enough for a jacket, but I don't have one and neither does she. If I had one, I'd offer it to her, but she probably wouldn't even take it.

"Skylar. It's Sean. Me. Sean," I plead.

"What."

At her screen door, she swivels, lithe, on her toes. She has green eyes that glow like a cat's.

"So, did you hear?" I whisper, as if anybody is listening to me or her.

"Hear what?" she says.

"That guy died."

She stares at me with those green eyes.

Skylar was one of the smartest people in school. Last year, junior year, cocaptain of the Math Club, Mathlete geeks. But anything connected to Jimmy and she turned into any dumb girl, or, worse, she became someone I hardly knew at all. Once I thought I knew everything there was to know about her, even if a lot of it was boring, like how she loved maps because she was, as she described it, geographically challenged. Last year, before she was with Jimmy, we pored over a city map of Boston. She was fixated on going to college in Boston. She also loved Manhattan, particularly the Village, with its maze of streets. She'd study that pocket street map and we'd get lost anyway, but that was a great time, every time. That was before Jimmy. He hated Manhattan. Refused to ever go in, maps or no maps. Too many people. Too many losers. I don't know what I'm thinking. I pitch myself toward a beat-up lounger with damp cushions covered in leaves, even though her backyard is treeless. Mine has this oak with a tire swing. I won't let my dad take that swing down. Sometimes I still like to go back there. And my sisters' kids enjoy it when I give them rides on it.

Sometimes I still like it— I don't know what I'm thinking. I don't want to think. He's dead. That guy. Him. The one I watched being beaten with a baseball bat. I squeeze my eyes shut against his name, against seeing him, against Skylar, the tire swing, the stars. And in the black of my vision, in a flash red with blood, his eyes find mine, and he's screaming, begging in Spanish, English, grunting, gasping, animal sounds. He's on his knees in the grass, close enough I could touch his head. I don't. I watch. Do nothing to save anyone.

I'm shaking now. Crying. Stupid crying, as if that will help. I did nothing to save him, that's what hits me.

"That guy. That guy, Skylar. Don't make me say his name."

"Sean," she says, her voice quavering, "his name was Arturo Cortez."

She's shivering. Maybe I should go over to her. But that would be too weird. I'm already here, sunk in this dank lawn chair.

"What are we going to do?" she asks, staying near her house, as if afraid to come too close. "I couldn't get in to see Jimmy today. Saturday. I'm definitely going to see him Saturday."

Panic rushes into her voice. I just told her that someone died. She's talking about seeing Jimmy. I don't get it. I don't get any of it. I wish she'd just sit here with me and be quiet like we used to, work on catching stars like we used to, open our mouths and believe we could float starlight onto our tongues, catch stars.

"What's going to happen now?" she asks.

I search the sky, wishing I were out in the woods somewhere upstate, wishing the night was pitch-black except for a sky full of stars.

"Sean? Doesn't this change everything?"

"I don't know. I've been trying not to think about it."

"But now we have to?" she says, pacing toward me. "Don't we? Someone's dead—and what are we going to do? What is going to happen"—and her voice catches—"to all of us?"

I say his name to myself, "Arturo Cortez," like a prayer.

"Sean, talk to me. Do you remember his face? Do you remember how he looked? Do you remember—"

"I can't. Skylar. I can't. I can't."

"What?"

"Forget."

She sinks down onto the lawn chair.

"I miss him, don't you?" she says. "Jimmy, I mean."

Now I look at her, see her, perched near my feet, all in black against the night, shoulders hunched forward, curled within herself. "I don't know," I begin. "I don't think I miss him. I think I hate him. I think I hate myself because of him."

I try not to touch her with my muddy sneakers. But my legs are too long. I have to jerk them off the lounger, pull up straight. She looks so small. She shivers. Her eyes widen and darken to a mossy green. I wish I could hold her without it being weird.

My arms hang off the side of the chair, scrape the dirt. I attempt to fold them across my chest, across the back of my head. I feel body-worn, like after a hard-hitting practice.

Everything that makes me good at sports like football and baseball, my height, the length of my arms, my speed, makes me feel like an alien everywhere—except on the field. And this makes me think of the game on Sunday. It's up in the air whether the school is going to let me play, or Jimmy if he gets out on bail. It's the last regular-season game of my high school career, and I want to play. Yet I never want to swing a bat again.

Skylar tilts her head back as if catching stars in her mouth. That's what we would say as kids, we were catching stars.

A smell of flowers drifts back here, though there are only buds, not flowers, anywhere. Her mother had a lot of flowers, roses, tulips, and I don't know what else, and it drove my mother up the wall, like they were in a flower-planting contest. Even Skylar, I realize, has a hint of flowers on her.

"You're not going to talk, are you?" she asks.

"I don't know."

"You have to know, Sean. It matters a lot."

I tilt my head back too. "Don't you think it was wrong? Don't you think that hurting someone for no reason like that is wrong?" No stars fall into my mouth. It's dry and empty and hanging open until I clamp it, swallow hard. "And we hurt him so bad that he's dead."

"Nobody meant to hurt anybody."

"What if Jimmy meant it that night? He did more than chase them and knock them down, and since I was there and did nothing about it, didn't I mean it too? This is what I've been thinking." I sink back.

"What do your parents say to do?"

"Say nothing. Let the lawyer get me off. I'm only seventeen. But I don't know—"

"You don't know what?" she says, in a voice so low I have to bend toward her. "What were you thinking that night? I won't tell anybody. But I need to know for myself what happened, what you and what Jimmy were thinking. Were you afraid?"

"Afraid?"

"Did something happen that made you, or even Jimmy, afraid— that made you get out of the car like you did?" She looks at me hopefully. I wish I could say that I was afraid that night. I wasn't. And I'm pretty sure Jimmy wasn't either. I don't even remember exactly what was said between us and—does it matter? I was afraid of nothing. I didn't think. We didn't discuss it. It didn't happen like that. I was watching, there, next to Jimmy, excited, jumping out of my skin. It all happened with one swing of the bat—

"Sean, you can't be the only one to talk."

Her hair blows against my forearms. I tense. Who else is going to talk? You, Skylar? You won't even admit that you were there.

Instead I say to her, "I don't know if I can lie for the rest of my life about what we did. I'm a really bad liar."

The moon frames her. I don't know what else to say. I wait for her to ask me something more, like, why didn't I stop him? Instead, she wraps her arms around me.

Coach Martinez
Football and baseball coach

I cut. Right through the head of Jimmy Seeger at the Scholar-Athlete award ceremony. With my school-issued scissors. Pieces of him scatter on my otherwise stark, clean desk. I'm in my office, door always open, right off the boys' locker room. The newspaper scraps make a nice mound.

I was hired here only to give this school bragging rights. Back in the day, I played a half a season with the Mets. Most of my career was in the minors. Kingsport, Tennessee; Norfolk; Savannah, Georgia; Port St. Lucie, Florida. I was decent. A pitcher for most of my career. Great for one year. Never had a problem with any of my teammates, any of my coaches. Got along with everybody until I met Jimmy Seeger and his father.

I was the first in my family to graduate college—from the University of Florida at Gainesville, which I attended on a baseball scholarship and graduated from in the mid-nineties. Went into teaching because I like kids and love the game and needed a job other than baseball at age thirty. Have two degrees, one in physical education and one in secondary school education. Grew up in Corona. In Queens. Flushing Meadows Park. Where the globe sculpture from the 1964 World's Fair is. Where the Lemon Ice King of Corona is. Where Shea Stadium was until they tore it down and replaced it. Used to park myself with three or four other guys in my crew on the Number 7 bridge over Roosevelt Avenue and watch the Mets games and sell bottles of water to all those folks panting in the sun. If it was very hot, we charged them double. If it was the playoffs, the World Series, triple. Not that we had a lot of those opportunities. Lived in a house right off the park with my father and mother and aunts and uncles and cousins and anyone else who was coming over or visiting for a time. Corona is less than an hour from this high school. You don't even have to drive over a bridge or pay a toll, but man, it's another world.

Last year, I jumped at this job. Why not? Thought the kids would be kids. Most of them are good kids. They wanted to play ball. My specialty is, of course, baseball.

I should have known something was up. I should have cut through the sports and seen it.

In the fall, I pitched in with the football team when the regular coach, Dan Davenport, who has been here for thirty years, had an emergency hernia operation. Davenport had given Seeger the quarterback position even though he was new to the school. He had a great arm, Davenport said. His former coach from Montauk, an old friend of Davenport's, said he was brutal and determined on the field.

But Seeger lost us the Turkey Bowl. He knew better than anybody, better than me, how to play his position. Threw right instead of left. Ball got picked off. Then he accused me of giving him the wrong signal.

In the locker room, I attempted to make something of the loss. It was a big loss, but we had a winning season. "Sometimes you learn from your losses," I remember saying to the team after that game.

From the back of the locker room, Seeger shouted out, "You know what you learn from losing, Coach? You learn from losing that you're a loser. And I won't believe that. You're giving us the wrong signal. Again."

I lost them then to Seeger. The team surrounded him in a snap of towels, a trampling of yips and howls. Looking back, I should have insisted we could and would learn from our mistakes, that it's not just about being winners or losers, it's about being a team, about working together, and sometimes winning, and sometimes, yes, losing. But I was mad at the loss too. So I left them to their showers and graces and stuffed turkeys.

I was determined with the baseball season to show him and all the others how to respect a coach—and win a championship. Called his old coach out in Montauk directly. He said, "Here's the thing about Seeger and baseball. Bottom line, he's a decent player and one of these guys everyone else likes to follow. Problem is his father thinks he should be the next Ty Cobb, you know him? And the kid sometimes thinks the rules don't apply to him. Last year, he was caught spiking another player sliding into second base. Happened to be a Hispanic kid. Bottom line is I want to win. But not like that. Anyway, I got no more to say about Seeger. I'm sure you'll do right by him."

I tried. We were on the way to a winning baseball season, maybe the best in a decade for the school. I gathered them around the locker room. They were kids like any other kids. Sure, I may have heard rumors about some of them going a little wild on the weekends. As long as they showed up on time and ready to play, was what I told myself. I wanted to win. I was going to inspire them. We were going to work hard, pull together, and win. Dressed and ready for practice, we could smell the fields ready for us with fresh-cut grass. They were tense, swinging bats, pounding balls into gloves. So I gave them a quote from a truly great baseball player, which I carried in my wallet, and which always made me work a little harder. " 'There are only two places in this league. First place and no place,' and I want us to end up in first place, what do you say?"

Seeger studied me. He had his one leg up on the bench. He was in the center of the boys. "I like that. Good stuff, Coach," he said, as if I had asked for his approval.

"What place do we want to end up in?" I said seriously, making sure I looked into the eyes of every player. It was like a dare with Seeger. Who would break off first? He had a soulless gleam in those blue eyes. I had to get practice going, so I did, but not until I repeated the quote, louder, and they responded with, 'First place. Or no place.' It became our motto, our cheer, before every game.

But Jimmy Seeger showed me no respect.

At the Scholar-Athlete ceremony, he insulted me. Ducked off when I offered him my congratulations, my hand. I smiled then. Filed it away. In the back of my mind where I put dirty players, the ones who head-butt or use steroids because they need an "edge."

I swipe the mound of Seeger's cut-up head off my desk. Class is in exactly fifteen minutes. And I never leave this office without a clean desk.

Bottom line, Seeger had a short swing. No patience. Whacked at the ball, and because he was lucky, or more lucky than the pitchers throwing at him, he hit it more times than not. Then he stopped connecting with the ball. All spring, he was in a slump. He couldn't hit. It made him hate the world even more. He felt like he wasn't lucky or special, like he was another dumb kid flapping at the ball. I know because I've been there, went through a few slumps when I was in the minors. By the third game of the season, I had to put his best friend, Sean Mayer, into the cleanup spot, Seeger's spot.

His father wanted him to play baseball more than he did—that much was clear to me. His father came to every practice. And with him there, Jimmy couldn't hit anything. His father screamed, *Eye on the ball, eye on the ball,* though one has to sense the ball, swing at it before you see it. Jimmy needed to keep his wrist tight and aligned. Had to snap his wrist. Had to keep his hands up. You need to be in control, not just have the appearance of control, not only a tight grip, but loose and tight at the same time, controlled inside as well as out.

I stepped in and showed him how to smooth the swing out, glide into the ball. The son didn't pay attention; the father did. The father called his son a sissy and a faggot when he missed. I had to say that we didn't use that kind of language here. I felt like some woman saying that, but those were the rules. After that, his father bought him a half dozen new bats so he could decide which one was his lucky bat. I heard he may have used one of those bats—

I stab the scissors into the top of my desk. And take a deep breath. Loosen the scissors, slip them into my desk drawer, and see the recommendation.

Sean Mayer. Before this whole thing blew up, he asked me to write a special recommendation to the baseball coach at the University of Florida, a man I knew very well. Sean was out there doing what he was doing, him and Jimmy Seeger and who knows how many others in this school, apparently it wasn't a secret, and had the balls to ask me for a recommendation as a walk-on. Then this week, after his arrest, his mother had phoned me to see if

I would still write a recommendation, saying it was more important than ever. I bet it was.

I'm waiting for Jimmy Seeger's father to call. In fact, last Friday, the day before what everybody around here is calling "the incident"—because we all know it's better to speak in code—his father showed up at practice. Insisted I pitch to his son. He wanted a "major league" pitch, he said.

I didn't want to. It wasn't my style to show up the kids.

But Jimmy's dad wouldn't take no for an answer. He followed me into the equipment room. He wasn't allowed in there and I told him so. He stood in the doorway, swinging his cane like a bat. "Come on, Coach. Let Jimmy show you what he's learned."

So we went back outside to the school's dedicated baseball field, the one with the electronic scoreboard. The one that always makes me think how, back in Corona, we swung our fathers' or older brothers' borrowed, well-worn bats and balls and mitts. We played every day after school until the park lights shone and people of the night, the ones we knew better than to talk to, circled the park benches.

Out there, on the grass, I pitched Jimmy a fastball, not my fastest, but certainly respectable. He had a major league stance. He pulled back the bat with grace. He sensed the ball more than he saw it. He had been practicing what I had taught him.

Seeger swung at my high fastball with pure anger. A good swing, a red-blooded swing, as Ty Cobb might have said.

Though I should have struck Seeger out. I should never have shown him how to swing a baseball bat with so much confidence that he could swing it anywhere. I jumped out of his ball's path.

Both father and son laughed. "Look at him dance," shouted

the father, or the son. They sounded alike: brazenly full of themselves.

"Happy now?" said the son to his father, or me, I wasn't sure. "Pitch me another."

I let another fly.

It was wild. Not on purpose, perhaps. Maybe I was out of practice with my major league fastball.

"I could report you for a pitch like that. You almost took my son's head off. Almost beaned him. What do you say? Don't say anything. My son was right. You have a bad attitude, Martinez. You don't belong here. I want my son back in the cleanup position."

"Let's see if he hits like that on Sunday," I said to the son, ignoring the father.

Jimmy shot me a look that said he'd show me. He'd hit that ball out of the park. I thought to myself then, good for him. If he has that motivation, I'll put him back in the cleanup position. I'll give him another chance. I want to believe in my kids. I want to be their coach, the one that they'll remember to their kids. But most of all, I want to win.

On Sunday, Seeger missed the game. Arrested. The news quoted his father saying that he was a Scholar-Athlete, the star of the varsity football and baseball teams, someone who worked well with others, including his coach. This time they made sure to include my name in the article.

I stand up. Look out my window at the absolute luxury of green fields surrounding this high school. I have learned that in the town next to this, their high school is looking for a new athletic director. The pay is less. But I have applied for the position. Right now I want to concentrate on one thing—ending the year with the best baseball season in the history of the school. I want to win the last game of the season even without Seeger, or maybe despite him.

Gloria Cortez

His face is a mask. I want to hide from this mask. It reminds me of the men that scorched the coffee bean fields my father worked. They too had impenetrable faces. Faces of stone. But this man is too young to be one of those men. This man with his white-ghost skin could be my son, except for the skin. He issues my name.

I have been in this airport room all night with no food, no water, nothing but dust. The air hangs around me, stale, heavy, so hot I can barely lift myself to face this American. I have spent the night with my soul burning. I should have stayed with my sons. I should never have left them without a mother in a foreign country. I should never have been afraid to leave here.

"Señora Cortez," he says, an American speaking Spanish badly and slowly like a schoolboy. I approach him with my head held high. I must be brave for my sons. But I am alone and it is very difficult to be brave. He is wearing a black wool business suit, too warm for this country at any time of year, and shows me his official badge from the United States of America. I nod my assent as if I can read what it says.

I repeat his name but cannot say it like him. His blue eyes crinkle, but then the mask reappears.

He has my visa. He leads me through the airport. A baby cries. A man smokes one cigarette after another. Nobody comforts the baby. He is guiding me, this Mr. Jones, from the government of the United States of America, through the airport terminal. The baby's cries trail us, echoing down the crowded halls and stabbing into my heart.

Mr. Jones must help me board the plane like I am an old woman. My legs drag. My heart dies. I am seated in the first seat of coach class facing a wall.

"In New York," he informs me in a strained low voice, "you will need to contact the U.S. Department of Justice, or they'll contact you, don't worry. Justice is now involved in this case."

"Justice?" I strain to say the *j* like him so he will not think I am a stupid woman.

"You understand?"

I nod my head even though I do not.

His blue eyes scan the packed cabin. His fine thin lips grimace.

"Everything will be okay," he lies. "We just need to get you to Long Island."

I know he lies. Nothing will be the same. Nothing will be "okay," except Arturo. He will recover from this once I am there.

"There is to be a court hearing, Señora Cortez, and you will face the accused. You should think of what you will say. There will most likely be some media covering the hearing. You've become what they call a cause célèbre in certain circles. So be prepared."

All I want to do is see my sons. I will be with both of them soon. Thank God.

The plane is ready to take off. Mr. Jones must leave. I clutch both his hands. They are smooth, soft, cool. I can't bear to let him go. He straightens up. I wonder how he does not sweat in this funereal black suit. His face is blank as he hurries off the airplane.

The kind blond stewardess tells me to buckle my seat belt. I confess, I fumble with the metal. My hands are callused and clumsy. I gasp. Choke. Cry without the wetness of tears, for I do not want to bother the other passengers.

Yes, yes, I am asking myself, what will I say at this hearing? What words are there for such grief? What mother would know? And what is a "hearing"? Who will hear me? Who heard my sons?

Police Officer Healey
Local patrolman

Let's lay out the facts as we know them. Last Saturday night at approximately 11:55 p.m., two Hispanic males, Arturo Cortez, age twenty-four, and his brother, Carlos Cortez, age seventeen, were reportedly assaulted. Carlos Cortez reported the incident to a 911 operator at approximately 12:15 a.m. Response time by police and ambulance was slightly longer than average but within department parameters. Both brothers were transported to the county hospital. Carlos was treated for minor bruises and released. Arturo Cortez suffered multiple blows to his head and body. He died from those injuries last night. The key question is, will anyone be charged with murder?

I cough. Clear my throat. I feel like I'm choking. I gulp down lukewarm coffee. I shove a doughnut, a plain one, into my mouth, push the crumbs off my desk. I pick back up the Cortez case file and continue. I have not been able to reach Mrs. Cortez. According to the embassy, she was placed safely on a plane to New York at approximately ten a.m. local time.

We have two high school students, including one James Seeger, Jr., age eighteen, honor student, star of the high school football and baseball teams, and Sean Mayer, age seventeen, son of the head of the Board of Education, initially charged with various counts of assault based on the testimony of Carlos Cortez, who is at best a questionable witness. We do not have anyone else to corroborate his testimony. We have no weapon. Is this case indicative of a pattern of hate-crime violence in our community? We have no record of such a pattern. Yes. That is correct. All other information regarding this case is above my pay grade.

Off the record, did we hear that there were a bunch of stupid kids harassing Hispanics on the street corners, raising a ruckus, causing some trouble? Yeah, maybe we did.

But nobody reported anything. If one of these Hispanics even entered the precinct, and maybe one or two did venture in, then we couldn't even get their names straight. Everybody was named José. We asked them for details: Who beat them up? What did they look like? What identifying feature? Did you get a license plate? Oh, right, they were on bicycles? What kind of bicycles? What proof did they have that they were beat up by kids or that they weren't in some bar in some fight somewhere? But we get nowhere.

And if off the record we asked them if they're foreign nationals, which really means are you here legally or not, they shut up and they ask to leave. I don't know what they expected us to do for them. I admit, it would have helped if we had a few more people in the precinct who spoke Spanish, or at least one at all times.

I have to backtrack. There was one report. About a month ago, two men came in to file charges. They claimed to have been attacked by boys wielding baseball bats. They were able to mime this to me. I kidded around with them, asked if they were Yankees or Mets fans. Not bad guys, I could see that if no else around here could. They got that I was trying. In fact, they were Yankees fans. I didn't hold that against them.

There was no one around who spoke Spanish and I knew I could call my wife and at least be able to communicate through her, though that is not official procedure and I tend to like to follow the book. These were young guys, early twenties. One had a broken arm, a knocked-out tooth. The other had stitches down the side of his face, he had a mustache. I could see that they hoped I could give them some justice.

My wife's name is Gracie, but she is also Graciela. She was born Graciela, and her family is from Puerto Rico, but I don't like to advertise that. When I introduced her to my family, over twenty-five years ago, I introduced her as "Gracie." We got engaged right away. It wasn't until the church wedding, when my jabber-mouthing Irish relatives had a bulb go off that Gracie's family were all speaking Spanish to each other, that it hit them that she wasn't Italian, which was bad enough for them. Not that this case has anything to do with Gracie.

It was my job to take the complaint. In broken English these two, José and José, attempted to describe to me what happened at the edge of town, near the bus stop, not far from the occurrence with Arturo Cortez and his brother. Like I said, I even joked with them, the Josés—so you're Yankees fans, you think they're going to go all the way? To the World Series again? There's something about sports, especially baseball, that transcends all of our differences, even language, if we let it.

That case is still open. No one has been charged. We are not even sure a crime took place.

Back to the case at hand. The case of Arturo Cortez. Will there be a murder charge? We have a dead body. But no weapon.

One more new development. Carlos Cortez has apparently placed the car of Skylar Thompson at the scene of the crime. His lawyer did us the favor of pointing this out to us. His description does match the Mustang Miss Thompson and her father drove away in the other day. However, Cortez could not give up a license plate number for that Mustang. Must be a lot of red Mustangs driven by pretty girls on Long Island. That's what their lawyers will say. No weapon. Nobody talking. It's going to be difficult if not impossible unless someone comes forward to get to the truth of the matter.

I got to say, Seeger and Mayer, they're neighborhood kids. Where were their parents? Or the schools? Or, Jesus Christ—

The captain is asking me to volunteer for an interfaith ceremony to be held on Saturday to bring together the community in the wake of this event. I wonder if there will be trouble.

Off the record, when I was a kid we had too much time on our hands. But we never set out to beat anybody up. We smoked pot and listened to the Beatles and the Who on our stereos, so that will tell you how old I am. We were too mellow, too stoned, too indifferent, in a way, to make this kind of trouble. Maybe that's the problem. We let the world go and we find ourselves here—arresting high school kids for assault, though now the ringleader, one Jimmy Seeger, may be charged with murder. What a waste. What a crime.

And too many pretty girls driving red Mustangs, unless one turns and talks.

FOR IMMEDIATE RELEASE TO MEDIA

INTERFAITH PRAYER VIGIL PLANNED FOR THIS SATURDAY

Clergy members and their congregations from our community are invited to attend an interfaith prayer vigil. Our community's faith-based institutions will gather this Saturday morning to discuss ways in which we can and should bring our neighboring towns together through prayer.

"We need healing and we need justice," said the Rev. Manuel Gonzalez of the Ark of Peace Assembly, who is hosting the event. "But we start with coming together in prayer at this critical time."

Gloria Cortez, mother of Arturo Cortez, who remains in critical condition at County Hospital, the latest victim of racial bias in our community, is expected to attend the prayer vigil on Saturday as well as key county and government officials. The public is invited to attend. All are welcome.

Please, please, please, let his mother answer the phone.

I'm in the Mustang, on my cell, parked out in front of my house, in the shade of the oak tree. I had put off calling, and now it's Thursday afternoon. I have to call if I'm going to see Jimmy on Saturday, alone.

Please, please, let his mother answer the phone. His mother, I chant. Only his mother.

"Hello! Who's this?" squeaks Grant's voice. "Dad, I don't know who it is." The phone clatters to the floor.

Not his father. Not him. I can't talk to his father. This is too hard. Thing is, he never talked to me. He's worse than my own father. Usually Jimmy's father pretended I wasn't there. I'd drop Jimmy off and he'd be staring out the window at us, just staring, never waving, never opening the door and saying hello. A stone-cold stare. I never called Jimmy's house. I had my cell, he had his. His father won't understand why I have to see Jimmy alone. Even more, I can't talk to him. According to Jimmy, before 9/11 he had a good job in construction before the Mexicans moved in on the jobs, working nonunion under the table, undercutting everyone, his father most of all. Now he can't work. He's on disability. Except for the cane he used outside the house, I never saw anything wrong with him. Jimmy said the 9/11 damage was inside as much as out, seeing what he had to see, doing what he had to do every day.

Last Thursday night, I desperately wanted to talk only about us, and it was so hard for Jimmy, he had so much on his mind all the time. We were lying next to one another in my bed. I said, "Let's talk about our trip. Our summer. The boat? Your grandmother's boat? Or graduation night? What we have planned?" My fingertips touched his face. I never made the first move. Never. What I really wanted was for him to kiss me and never stop.

"Okay," he said. "I think I'm just going to take Sean out with me on Saturday night."

"Maybe I could come sometime?" I had never suggested this before. I didn't really want to go. He always had a no-girls rule.

"Nah," he said, flipping on his side, grabbing my waist, tickling me until it hurt and I was crying, begging him to stop. When he fell back, I tried to kiss him.

He wouldn't have it. It was as if he knew that I wanted more than kisses, more than touches, maybe even wanted to break his rule of tops off, bottoms on. He said that he had to save me from myself and held my arms back and gave me one kiss on the cheek and said it was time for him to sleep. We had planned graduation night, in Montauk, on the beach as our first real night together. He had said he wanted it to be special. He had wanted it to be forever. Even more, he said, always gently, he wanted to make sure I had grieved for my mother in the proper way, not by rushing into sex. He could control himself and so should I. I was pure. This was real; though he didn't use the word *love,* I added it in my head. The rest of the world may be out of control, he said, the poor or the illegals, leeches, or whatever, on our borders, I don't remember the rest. But according to Jimmy, we together could make it right. I just had to control myself. I had to wait. My heart lurches, remembering.

Was that only last Thursday night?

On the other end, someone grabs the phone. I brace myself. All I have to say is, *I'd like to see Jimmy alone.* I don't have to say anything about the bond or the charges or anything else. Someone clears his voice. His father, like Jimmy, is over six feet, fiercely blue-eyed. His face is raw and veined and framed by prematurely white hair. He used to play baseball like Jimmy, in high school too, I think.

"Skylar Thompson," the voice roars. "I'm glad you called. I was going to call you."

"I wanted to ask you, Mr. Seeger—"

"I want you, Skylar, to go visit Jimmy this Saturday. By yourself. He needs to see you. He needs to know you're on his side. He needs to talk to you. We all got to be in this together, Skylar, if we want Jimmy out, and we want him out. That is a question. We want him out?"

I am mesmerized by the voice. It's Jimmy's voice, deeper, tougher, though with "dem" for *them,* and "der" for *there,* and "dis" for *this.* That's the Brooklyn in him, common enough around here, but starker on Mr. Seeger, like a badge of honor. I reply with a faint, "Yes."

"Good girl. You'll visit on Saturday. Wear something nice. When I went there this week all the girls were dressed up. Brings up the morale."

"I will."

"Can you do this?"

Like Jimmy, he makes me think I can do anything.

"Jimmy's a winner. Remember that. There are winners and losers. Don't even think that just because one of them decided to die it changes anything. Changes nothing."

Wait a minute. Doesn't it change everything? The older brother is dead. Jimmy can be charged with murder. I feel light-headed.

He keeps on answering his own questions. "Nothing. He is guilty of nothing. Nothing. Except maybe, maybe being in the wrong place at the wrong time. Did you know they found a knife on that guy? And we only have the word of one dropout loser, one loser's loser, against my son and his friend. And we're going to keep it that way, aren't we, Skylar Thompson?"

That's what we all thought, didn't we? There were winners and losers in the world and we wanted to be winners, didn't we? We had to make our own rules, didn't we? And we could do anything. It's a strange, warped, ugly equation from his father; it was never that way with Jimmy. I have to see Jimmy. I grip the cell. Why does he think that this won't change things? Why? I'm sure Jimmy will be devastated—someone is dead—and he was there—something happened that night. Stop. "There was a knife, Mr. Seeger?"

"Yup," he says. "The cops got it. Might be on the news tonight, though I think this story should be old news by now."

I didn't see a knife, did I? But that doesn't matter. Jimmy must have seen it. Maybe Arturo Cortez hid it until he was right up against the SUV. He must have threatened Jimmy and Sean. I mean, Jimmy shouldn't have shouted out to him and his brother like he did. But it wasn't what Jimmy believed; it was only what he said. Everyone knew that. It was never supposed to be this way. No one was ever supposed to get hurt like this, dead-hurt.

"Listen, Jimmy needs one thing from you. You know what that is? He needs you to believe in him."

"Mr. Seeger?"

"Yes?"

I feel like there's an immeasurable space between us. My head hurts. I'm so glad there was a knife, I mean, relieved. I'm glad I talked to Jimmy's father. I want him to like me. But I need to go. I don't know where, but I need to drive somewhere. Now. Go.

"Have a good night, Mr. Seeger."

"My son will rise above this, you'll see." *Click*. Dead air.

Skylar Thompson

Thunderclouds are strung across a blue-black sky. It's prematurely dark. It should be that time of day when the heat magically drifts away, but it doesn't. Even with the wind blowing, the heat bears down. There's no shade. Plastic bags fly like bloated feathers across the turnpike. The only hope is for a storm. I skid off the turnpike.

I don't know how I drove around for hours after talking with Jimmy's dad and found myself here, about ten, eleven minutes from my house. But I'm here. I believe in Jimmy. But I'm back here.

Here is nowhere. It's a stretch of road between towns. It's this restaurant, a last outpost. A field. A bus stop. And just like last Saturday night, I swing into the parking lot of the barbecue place, head around the back and to the corner of the other side. I have a perfect view of the turnpike, its four lanes: two going south, two north, a concrete island in between.

This afternoon, meat is cooking, smoking the air. This is a family-style restaurant, its specialty—slabs of ribs. My father always used to suggest going here, before my mother got sick. We never did. Now a confusion of scents find their way through my open car window: ozone, meat-grease, car exhaust. I peel my hands from the wheel, let my head fall back.

I'm here. South of the bus stop, the neighborhood changes as if by some agreement, and there's no reason for me to ever go there except when my father takes one of his famous shortcuts off the L.I.E. On that side of the border, stores are boarded up. Office buildings are hung with FOR RENT signs. The stores that are open, we never go in them. They offer check-cashing and money-wiring with signs in English and Spanish. That always prompts my father to say something absentmindedly like, 'Don't they know we speak English here?' Men stand in small groups on corners, though there is always a deserted quality to the streets.

I struggle to sit up. I shake my head as if I've been asleep. Next to the barbecue restaurant is no-man's-land. It's a vacant lot, a field. Waist-high grass is strewn with plastic bottles and beer cans, and, I notice now, bunches of improbably lovely yellow wildflowers. The bus stop, indicated by a metal sign posted to a telephone pole, is in front of the field. No bus shelter. A spot on the shoulder of the turnpike, that's all. When Jimmy and Sean chased them, they ran from the bus stop across those fields. I heard the screams from out there in the grass. Now, next to the faded FOR SALE billboard on this strip of undeveloped land, a police barrier has been put up, right next to the wildflowers.

Thunder rolls. Clouds are swift overhead. My heart jumps. I shouldn't be here. That's not what I said that night, was it? I was thrilled to be here.

That night started out like any other Saturday night. We had met up at my house. My father was working like always.

"It's his drug. Work," explained Lisa Marie in her know-it-all psychoanalyst tone. Then she offered around the latest from her mother's medicine cabinet. I didn't partake; I never did. Neither did Jimmy; he had a beer or two. Sean, of course, had no problem taking one pill of each color and washing them down with vodka.

Lisa Marie was making eyes at Jimmy, but I ignored her and so did he, or at least I want to think he did. No, I'm sure he did. We were having a good time, that's all.

Everyone was meeting up at the Dunkin' Donuts at the far corner of the town shopping center, in the back parking lot, along the tree edge, our go-to place. Last week, Benny, whose family runs the Dunkin' Donuts, really wanted to be part of Jimmy's crew. His family is from Bangladesh. As Jimmy liked to point out, his family is here legally. That's different. And they always gave us free doughnuts. And no one bothered us at the back of the lot.

When we all convened, there must have been at least twenty of us. Benny ran out with flat boxes of doughnuts and had to make apologies. His father needed him in the store. He couldn't be considered for the crew that night or even stay for more than a minute. He knew enough to bring out Jimmy's favorite, coconut-crusted, and Jimmy promised he'd be on the list next time. He washed down a half dozen doughnuts with two Red Bulls. Benny was thankful. He couldn't stop saying thank you. That annoyed Jimmy enough that he started imitating Benny.

Everybody laughed, even me. I laughed even though I knew it hurt Benny.

Even though he looked at me with the saddest eyes, I laughed. He looked at me as if me laughing were what was wrong with the world. I didn't think that then, but I do now.

Benny raced back into his parents' store, and Jimmy announced his plans. Only Sean and him this time. Next week, members of the baseball team, after the last game of the season. He winked at me.

I knew what he was doing. By excluding the others he made them want to join him even more. Sean was jumping up and down like a puppy, a drunk, high puppy, scampering at Jimmy's side, saying, "Let's go. Let's go! *Let's go!*" Like a cheer, like I don't know what.

Jimmy said that the rest of us would "reconnoiter"—how he loved to use those kind of words, as if we were all speaking in our own secret language. We'd meet up in everyday language back here by midnight. Grumbling, dissent, noise ensued. Everyone wanted to be picked.

Last Saturday night. I wasn't with Jimmy in Sean's SUV. I can honestly claim that. He didn't even know that Lisa Marie and me had followed him and Sean. But I was here, desolate here, nowhere, meaningless without Jimmy—

And then I see him. The other brother. The one who ran through the field. He's angling across the parking lot of the barbecue restaurant. How could I ever come back to this spot? How could he?

My head pounds. I need air. Of course, he never saw me or the Mustang before. I'm nobody to him. Nothing. Even so, I don't dare move.

He's dressed in black pants and a white button-down shirt. He has a face made of right angles, sharp high cheekbones. Long arms jut out of sleeves that need to be longer. He's taller somehow. Or maybe his black hair is shorter, or just slicked tight off his face. It was dark last Saturday night. No, that's not right. There was a full moon. Anyway, I was focused on Jimmy.

I should go. But now that I'm here, I mean, there must be some reason I'm here. That night, I had to see for myself what was what with Jimmy and his excursions. It wasn't that I didn't trust him, but I had to see for myself. And I thought it would be fun. I feel the same compulsion now, without the fun part.

A roly-poly fat man blunders out of the barbecue place.

He's calling out, "Carlos."

And Carlos tenses. He raises a square-cut chin defiantly, but then smiles what looks like a forced smile, I mean, the smile is not in his eyes, which are narrowed, more black than brown, zeroed on the fat man.

"Carlos, man." The fat man huffs over to Carlos. "My uncle wanted you to have this." He hands Carlos a big shopping bag from the restaurant. "He said you don't got to show up for the next few days. Everyone was surprised that you were here today, man."

"I don't work, I don't get paid, right, Angie?" asks Carlos lightly. He has no accent. He sounds like any kid from Long Island.

The fat man says nothing.

Carlos takes the shopping bag from this sweating, pink-skinned man. "I'll see you tomorrow, Angie."

"Yeah," says Angie, as if digesting this idea, before flopping two steps back toward the restaurant. He stops, wheezes, shouts, "Hey, Carlos. I almost forgot. One more thing. We're not going to get into any trouble with anybody coming around questioning us about your status or nothing? We heard your brother was taking all kinds of jobs using a fake Social Security number. We don't need any trouble—"

"I was born here," he says without raising his voice. "That means I'm American like you, Angie. Anybody come around and check your status?"

"Yeah, that's right," he says slowly, as if this is a big thought for him. "It's just that, man, even my uncle is worried these days about the government coming around and checking things, if you know what I mean, man. But hey, don't worry, Carlos, you're different. I'm sorry about it all, man. You are good people."

"See you tomorrow, Angie," Carlos replies flatly, waiting until Angie backs off, until he lumbers toward the cooking meat, before continuing on.

I don't know what to think. Jimmy was always saying that these people come here and are ungrateful, living off of us like leeches. Except Carlos has a job. A dead brother and a job.

That night Lisa Marie was passed out. I can honestly say that. She was out, curled up in the passenger seat, happy, stone-cold out. We were in this parking lot, headlights off, at the far corner of the restaurant too close to these exhaust vents, hidden.

I was thinking that maybe I could be the type of girl who did wild or risky things, that I'd like to be that type of girl, that that's the kind of girl who'd always be Jimmy's girl. I was thinking that and watching as Jimmy, on the passenger side, stuck out his arm, gesturing for them to come over by flicking the air with his fingers.

The older one, Arturo, shorter, bulkier, had his arm draped over the younger one. He swung free and approached the SUV alone. Jimmy motioned for him to come even closer, even closer still, and grabbed his forearm—they were only supposed to bean them with a scuffed-up baseball, knock them to the ground or make them run.

Those were Jimmy's rules for his crew. He always said that he wanted to scare them off, make it a game, nobody wanted them in our town, or at the edge of our town, or even here in no-man's-land. It's a small island, that's what Jimmy always said.

Arturo must have been strong. He wrenched free from Jimmy.

That must have made Jimmy mad. Before I knew what was happening, Arturo was screaming in Spanish. He was running, pulling Carlos, the doors to the SUV flew open.

Jimmy out with a bat, his bat. Sean was following, roaring, "Go, go, go. Let's go." And Jimmy was cutting through the field. *Go. Go. Go.*

I thought you'd both get away.

I saw the bat swing. I heard it—*crack*. Your brother struck across the back of his head. *Crack.* I heard it as much as saw it. That's all. I swear.

I took off. I careened the Mustang in the opposite direction. Jimmy and Sean never saw my Mustang race out of there. I sped down this strip of turnpike faster than I ever drove in my life. Lisa Marie didn't even stir.

Streetlights are broken. Were they that night? Unseen birds call to one another frantically. Ozone chokes the air. The sky grows more black than blue.

Hey, Carlos, I want to call out. *I want to talk to you.* I want to, but I can't. I can't even move. I can't talk to you, can I? What could I possibly say that would mean anything to you? "Hey, Carlos," I whisper. I know you can't hear me. You're at the bus stop, looking over your shoulder, glancing side to side, and toward the restaurant. I'm over fifty yards away. You can't see me. You don't know me. *I don't know you,* I want to scream out. You didn't see me that night. Nobody did. Nobody knows I was there except for my father and Lisa Marie. You glance up and down the turnpike. You must be looking for the bus. You're not hitchhiking. Please. I mean, I don't even know where they go. Buses. I don't know anyone who rides them. I mean, I've been on school buses. Up until last year I rode a school bus every day of my life. I mean every school day. Everyone in our district takes a bus. You can live a block from school and get picked up by the bus. I never understood that. But that's the school policy. I don't think parents want their kids walking to school. There're all sorts of predators around today. I mean perverts. But where would this bus take me if I got on? Would it go all the way down to the beaches? I bet it does. They're really not far, though sometimes you forget that. We live here on the island, a small island, and forget there are beaches. Last summer, I didn't get to the beach at all. I barely left the house. I was with my mother. We knew she was dying—of ovarian cancer—so I stayed with her. She always said her one thing in life beyond my father and me was her car. She liked sports cars. And she didn't even drive fast. She'd let my father drive fast in her car when it was just the two of them. That's what she said to me at the end, when she was pressing the keys into my hands. She said, "Let your father drive the car once in a while." But he never wants to drive it. I'm sorry. I am. About your brother. *Sorry* is a word to be pitied, that's what my mother always said. Nobody truly knows the true meaning of that word, she said. Better to focus on hope, she said. I hated anyone who said they were sorry about my mother's passing. Were they truly full of sorrow? Isn't that what *sorry* means? You know, I've been asked to give another statement. It was hardly a request. Police Officer Healey said it should take thirty to sixty minutes. Lisa Marie says that her father thinks I should get a lawyer if I go. She says I don't have to go, that I shouldn't say, do anything else unless I'm subpoenaed, and even then I can still say that I don't know anything about anything. It's true. I mean, I don't know anything anymore.

A police car passes. A plastic bag perches on my windshield. I have to drive away. I feel dizzy.

You see, I shouldn't be here now. Jimmy would hate me to be here. You got to know though, I would never call you a faggot or a homo, or a stinking Mexican, or a stupid beaner. I know what they said was worse, much worse, especially after the doors to the SUV flew open and Jimmy pounded after you with a bat. It was a clear night. I was listening and looking at every move and sound from Jimmy. If Jimmy knew you were brothers, he never would have called you faggots. But you were here, with your arms around each other. Honest, I've never heard him saying anything against homosexuals before. You got to know this, even though I can't speak to you, you see. I shouldn't be here now.

I tug my sweater tighter. I haven't eaten all day and that's probably why I'm cold. I have to go. I have to eat something. I mean, what can I say now? Nobody could say anything to me when my mother died. I have nothing more to say to anyone, except to Jimmy. No hope, I mean, except for him.

A screech of brakes.

A jolt of exhaust.

Twelve tires instead of four. Doors crank open. How much does it cost to ride? Passengers slant against one another, some standing, some sitting. Heads are in hands, a few babies, a few bulging bags on laps. You stand, in the center, as the bus grinds away

Carlos! Hey, Carlos!

If I say that I am full of sorrow, for your brother's death, I mean, would it matter now? A muddy darkness descends all at once. The stench of meat-burning and car exhaust swirls up. I retch. The sky rumbles. Rain bursts on this small island, and plastic bags, broken feathers, flatten on turnpikes.

Even at midnight, the international arrivals area of John F. Kennedy Airport is jammed with the world. Families yell greetings in a hundred different tongues. Men with thick mustaches offer rides. Luggage piles up waist-high and children run in between it all. The ceilings are low, the lighting poor, the floors scattered with candy wrappers and bottles of half-drunk water. It's airless. I've been sweating and pacing for the last two hours. Every five minutes, I check arrivals. I shake the flowers I have brought for her as if to keep them alive. Her flight, already hours late, delayed by thunderstorms, and delayed again on the runway for no reason at all.

The last time I was here, as a boy, my American passport hung around my neck like a talisman, a charm. At customs, I was sent to a different line. I was smiled at by the agent and waved on. My aunt, uncle, and Arturo met me. Arturo picked me up, held me aloft in his big arms until I squirmed down, and he chased me out the doors.

Tonight, everyone in the world is claiming a loved one. Another hour drags by. I want to lie down on the floor. Scream. Cry. I should have been with him. I should have taken the blows on my back. And I should have been in the hospital, when he died. I must be a man now. I must be here for her, and for Arturo. And I must be able to speak the truth to anyone else who will listen.

"Mami!"

I have brought white roses and eucalyptus because they are her favorite, because Arturo would have bought her these flowers, because he loved giving women flowers, for our aunt on holidays, for the girls at the *quinceañeras*. The bouquet is crushed in our embrace. My aunt and uncle circle my mother and me. They shed tears too. And watch over us as if we need extra protection. We are sobbing with a peculiar mix of grief and joy that leaves us grabbing each other, gasping for air, crying out for the dead as well as the living, engulfed in the bouquet's scent.

Soon, my uncle offers to get the car and bring it around. He doesn't want to pay a fortune in parking. He has been in this country for over thirty years and hates highway tolls and parking fees and the small ways the government wears down the workingman.

My aunt, always impatient, says, "Go, go, be useful. Go get the car. I'll get the bags. We don't want to spend all night here."

My mother's hair is bound up against her neck. I remember how, when I was young and still with her, I loved to brush out her waist-long hair. She'd bend down on her knees and guide my hand against her hair. After she sent me to Arturo, I once told her that I was worried about her hair, it was lonely without me. But she laughed and said don't worry, her hair was fine. She was always thinking of cutting it, threatening to use the money Arturo sent to go to the beauty parlor, but obviously she never did. Now I am taller than her by at least a foot. I am the one to bend and to burrow into her hair.

Mami.

Mami.

Mami.

White petals scatter on the dirty floors. The sweet smell of eucalyptus is pressed into my white work shirt, into her old-fashioned black cotton dress. My mother's arms tighten around me. "Forgive me," I say. "I couldn't save him."

She shakes me from her, stands me straight. "Look at me. What are you telling me, *papi?*"

"Now I am your only son."

We collapse into each other's arms.

Everybody knows. Nobody's talking.

That's my mantra. Nobody is talking. Everybody is looking to me to confirm this. And I do. Everybody knows. Nobody's talking.

Sean is like a celebrity this Friday morning in the school parking lot. The school had made it clear to him that he is still required to attend class to graduate in June. But there was never any question of him returning to class. He should be here. He broke no school rules.

It's one of those glorious June mornings when no one wants to be in class, not even the teachers. I'm in a sleeveless white tank and deep purple jeans that are perfect for the day. I lean against my black Camaro and feel like I'm glowing in the sun.

There's the final game of the baseball season this Sunday, and if we win, we go on to the county-wide playoff. "If Jimmy were going to play, we'd be guaranteed a win," boasts Jake Kroll, as if he were on the team.

"He's got his hitting back," says Benny. Some stupid, nervous laughs burst out from the edge of our crowd. I'm surprised at Benny, but then, he was always trying a little too hard. I ignore him.

Sean throws back his head, opens his mouth as if he's going to laugh, and doesn't. He pants as if he can't catch his breath. He punches his chest with his fist. I don't know what's going on with him. He smells rank like he hasn't showered since—I won't say it—I'm not going to think of him or Jimmy in jail—like he hasn't showered after a long practice in the hot sun.

I whack Sean playfully, but really not. "What is going on with you?"

"Easy," he says, panting.

I punch him harder. I want him to tell everyone to talk about something else, but he doesn't get it. Then suddenly he lets loose, laughing. I wonder if he's high. He really doesn't have much to worry about. He's a minor. His parents are taking care of everything. His mother even called my mother. He has nothing to worry about.

"You don't get it, do you?" Sean says to me, red-faced. "All year, all of us, all of us seniors, Lisa Marie, have been hoping for the year to end and never end. A break in time and space. Now every waking moment—because I don't sleep anymore—all I wish is that I could turn back time and have it be one week ago. Instead I'm hurtling through space."

"I get it," I say under my breath to Sean. Everybody knows: nobody's talking or making remarks or laughing about this incident as long as Jimmy is in danger. We have to be loyal.

"Think about Jimmy," I remind him.

He hangs his head. "I'm going home. And don't worry. Jimmy is all I think about."

"Sean, don't be a loser," I say, locking on to his forearms. He shrugs me off. "Sean, we should talk more about what you're feeling," I offer. I am overcome with frustration. All I want to do is make sure the incident is dealt with in the best way for everyone, including Sean, who by his own confession to me screwed up last Saturday night.

But I'm distracted. Skylar is shuffling across the parking lot to the senior spots. Everyone except Sean surrounds her. He is sprinting across the parking lot, darting between cars. I should go after him. But I'm sure he'll be fine. I'll work on him later. My focus right now needs to be Skylar. I'll get back to Sean. I have to keep everyone together, and obviously, Skylar needs me more.

Her hair is scrunched up on the back of her head. She's wearing a sweater and black T-shirt, the same thing as yesterday, and looks like she hasn't slept. I step forward, wrap her in a world-class Lisa Marie hug, though I want to shake her.

"Are you okay?" I whisper in her ear.

"No."

"Talk to me."

I expect her to say more. The first-period bell rings. I want her to say more. All of us are moving as one, slowly, the sun in our eyes, toward the open double door.

"What's happened?" I say, grabbing her arm.

"I have to talk."

"Talk to me. Let's cut first."

Skylar shakes her head, wades inside. Long, wide rivers of corridors, each with signs marked FRIENDSHIP WAY, COOPERATIVE DRIVE, KINDNESS COURT, as if they direct us instead of our raw instinct, converge here. A banner congratulating our class on graduation hangs between Friendship and Kindness. The bells shrill their last warning. I have to hurry to catch up to her, which pisses me off.

"What are you talking about 'talking'?" I say, cornering her by the showcase highlighting the spring play, *Rent: Student Edition*. I stare at a poster that shows drama club students dressed up as poor artists on the Lower East Side. A big hit. I loved it.

"Why hasn't anyone said something?"

"What? That we're sorry?" I say close up to her, trying to make her see reason.

"I hate that word," Skylar says. "What does it really mean?"

"It means nothing. There's nothing for us to be sorry for. You and I didn't do anything. And the boys are not guilty. Remember 'not guilty.'" Sometimes Skylar truly needs things spelled out for her.

"I'm being asked to come in for more questions. More? What more do they want to ask me? It's voluntary, but my father now wants me to have a lawyer, and you're going to hate me—"

"Never," I say to my oldest friend, "only if you talk—"

"I've been thinking more and more about them."

"Who?"

"Those brothers."

"Oh."

"Arturo and Carlos Cortez. Their family, what about them? We were there. We saw them taunting Carlos and Arturo. Chase them."

"I did not," I say, and this is the truth. I brush the hair away from her face. "Skylar. I saw nothing."

"That's right. You were passed out."

"I wasn't there, Skylar."

"You were passed out in the passenger's seat," her voice snapping after every other word. "Can't we at least be truthful with each other?"

"I wasn't there."

"Okay, you weren't there. But you knew where we were going. You knew as well as anybody, maybe better than anybody other than Jimmy, what was happening all year."

"I didn't, and I don't, know anything."

"Don't you at least think we should say we're sorry?"

"No."

Her sweater slumps off her slim quivering shoulders. I try to help her fix her sweater. She fumbles with the buttons. I button the top one for her. "We can talk about this somewhere else. This is not the place to talk about it."

"Where is? Not here. Not the police station. Where? I don't know where to go."

"Skylar, please." I hush her. The halls are rapidly emptying around us.

Her head falls to her chest. I can't see her face. I have to strain to hear her. "I saw. Jimmy had a baseball bat in his hands. I'm sorry." And then, unbearably, for I wish I had love like this, she says, "I still love him. I'm breaking apart. My heart is breaking. I mean, I'm starting to hate myself. But I love him."

I brush her hair away from her face. She can't look me in the eye.

"I have to go to class," she says. "I have a test. I'm sorry. I have to go—"

I don't let her by me. "Shut up, Skylar, please. Focus. Don't get me wrong, I know this is a nightmare; it's going to be a long night-mare for all of us. We need to support one another. They've pleaded not guilty. Everybody knows they weren't trying to really hurt anybody." How can I make her understand? She's mumbling something about a calculus test. I want to drag her out into the sun and make her understand: everybody knows; nobody is saying anything. Nobody. That includes me. That includes her.

"I'm going to help you, Skylar. I am. Please shut up. Be quiet. Come to me." I wrap my arms around her. She smells musty and mildewed and old. "Don't worry, Skylar. I'm going to be there for you. You understand that you are not alone in this? No one needs to say anything more to anybody. Nobody needs to talk about what was going on, or wasn't."

Skylar is pushing past me. So I say, "He called me too."

"Who?"

"Jimmy."

This stops her.

"What?"

"Before he called you, Skylar," I say in such an ordinary voice that I could be telling her to have a nice day.

This wakes her up.

"He's worried," I say. Finally, I have her attention.

"About me?"

I hesitate. "About everything." A lie of omission. "He asked me to take care of things, you know what I mean?"

"I'm not sure," she says, her shoulders rounding forward, like this is a test.

"Trust me."

"I don't think I trust anyone anymore."

"Are we going to class, Miss Thompson? Miss Murano?" asks Coach Martinez, approaching us on hall patrol. He's gorgeous. I don't care what nationality he is. See, doesn't that prove something? I want to say this to Skylar, but she's already shuffling, head down, toward her class.

"And you, Miss Murano? Class today?"

I swivel. I smile at the coach and murmur, "Spring fever," sliding my feet down the waxed floors as if I'm hurrying, though clearly I'm not.

I avoid looking at Mr. Lake, my calculus teacher, who's fussing with the test papers and squinting at me like he hates me. He wants to fail me and I'm helping him. He used to be my favorite teacher, the adviser to the math team.

He flicks the test paper at me. Everyone says that he lives with Mr. Schwartz, the music teacher. That he's gay. Not that I care if he's gay or not. But that's what everyone says. Both men are among the youngest teachers in the school, live off the island, in Brooklyn somewhere.

Numbers that have always been so consistent in my life don't seem to work anymore. I can't concentrate. *Jimmy called Lisa Marie too?* The equations jumble. I think I'd have a problem if someone asked me what two plus two is right now.

Everybody knew what Jimmy and Sean—and the others who joined them on other weekends—were doing when they said they were going beaner hopping. Nobody said it would lead to this. Nobody thought it was anything more than what it was. And now there's someone dead. And now the police want to talk to me again. I can't do it. I can't.

I leave an answer blank. Go on to the next one. Just keep going as if the right answer will come to me then.

Jimmy liked to plan where and when in more detail than the others knew. It was just a maneuver, he told them. No injuries intended, patrol tactics only. The United States was finishing construction on a wall to keep them out, he shared. Even our county was making extra efforts to round up and evict them, he pointed out.

He said he only needed a few good men. This is Jimmy talking. He liked to talk like he was already in the military. Two plus two always added up to four for Jimmy. He was so sure of who he was and what he had to do—he gave me confidence. Where would I be without him? After my mother died he was the only one who understood that I needed someone to listen.

Numbers scatter away from me.

Nobody thought that something like this could happen. Everyone wanted to be there with Jimmy. We'd meet up before and after and party, especially after. And I was suddenly at the center of it all, instead of the fringes, because I was Jimmy's girl.

Nobody thought the kids out here could do what they are accused of doing. I can't even watch the local news. I don't believe what they're saying. They're talking about other kids, not us. I put down my pencil. I stare at the scribbles and cross-outs and erasures on my paper. Jake Kroll eases his test toward the edge of his desk, as if giving me a chance to peek at his answers. I don't.

Nobody thought. But I did. I know. I was there. Wasn't I?

I raise my head; the room is empty. I'm the last one finished. As I shuffle to the front of the room to hand in my test, I notice that Mr. Lake's fingernails are bitten down to the quick. He snatches the test from me and throws it on his desk like it has a disease. He's going to fail me. I'm a senior. I shouldn't care. But I do. I have never failed any test before in my life. "Miss Thompson?" he says, cutting in between me and the door. "I need to talk with you."

I freeze.

"About calculus," he says, his gentle brown eyes searching for mine. "What is calculus?"

This wasn't on the test I just handed in.

He answers himself. "It is the exploration of two ideas, the derivative and the integral. It's an analysis of motion."

I stare at the floor. I repeat what he once said before a Mathlete tournament. I am as surprised as he is that I remember his words. "Calculus is the mathematical structure that lies at the core of the world of seemingly unrelated ideas."

"Exactly. I knew you couldn't have lost your mind these past few months. So apply it to life. My life. Yours. Someone is shamed. Called names. Beat up. Murdered, even." He presses closer and speaks faster. His left eye twitches. It would always twitch during the last round of any Mathlete competition, as if sending us signals. "We didn't call the name or wield the bat, so we believe on the surface that it is unrelated to us. If we understand the beautiful rationale underlying ideas of calculus as well as you do, can we believe that what's happened is unrelated to us?"

"Maybe the world isn't rational," I mumble, and hurry out of his classroom into the crowded hall.

I try to avoid the principal.

I want to run. I back against the wall and Mrs. Plotinsky steps in front of me. "Miss Thompson," she announces more than says. The crowd parts around us. She is wearing her customary black pants suit and chunky necklace from her closet of black pants suits and chunky necklaces. She has a way of cocking her head to the side to look at you without really seeing you. I wait for her to say more about Jimmy or last Saturday night or some lecture. Last September, she called me into her office with its wall of school heroes, photos from random school events, and said she wanted to offer her and the school's "help" with my loss. She urged me to talk with the school psychologist or social worker. I spoke with neither.

I wait for her to say something like that now, make an offer to meet, with her or the school psychologist or social worker. Maybe she'll want to have my father join us again. He'll have to say again that he can't make it, he's working. I resolve to say that I have no reason to meet or talk or confess to anybody, even though she must know like everyone else that I'm Jimmy's girl. Though, in some way, I thought the school would mobilize somehow after this incident, I mean, have an assembly or an after-school program or, at least, announce that there are counselors available to talk. But it feels more like it's on lockdown. *Everybody knows, nobody is talking.*

In front of me, the principal offers a tight smile to the air above my head.

I'm going to have to tell her again that I don't need any help.

Mr. Lake rushes toward us, his arm full of test papers. I think he'll stop, urge me to talk in front of the principal.

"Let's keep focused on school issues, shall we, Miss Thompson? Graduation is just three weeks away, and you're free," she says to me in the same way she would announce the day and weather over the loudspeaker. "You must be excited? I know I am," she continues, tilting her head toward Mr. Lake. He holds her gaze for a moment before breaking free, twitching his left eye only, waving the test papers as an excuse not to stop.

"Well, Miss Thompson," she says, not freeing me yet, not until she says something about Jimmy, I'm sure. But she doesn't say anything else to me, anything about help or Jimmy, or anything. She looks like she just wants to go. She tilts her head left and right, her necklace clunking against her chest, and latches on to a freshman on the baseball team. He's loping down the hall, and she announces to him that she'll be in the stands on Sunday, rooting for him and the team. Go team.

None of them know anything. The principal is working hand in hand with the police, or at least that's Lisa Marie's theory.

I'm talking to no one but myself. I'm telling myself: I'm here; I'm in the school's west wing, I'm running down the halls—and stop short at the sports award showcase. Jimmy's picture from the Scholar-Athlete award is missing. I press my face against the glass. All they want is for Jimmy to disappear. Who took the picture? I wish I could see him. My heart is breaking. Doesn't everyone know that my heart is breaking?

I avoid Lisa Marie. I cut out before lunch because I know she will be there waiting to "help" me. It's organic vegetarian day. The whole school smells like stewed tomatoes and onions. I hunker down past the cafeteria doors, past the kids wolfing down candy bars and chips from the snack machine. If I make myself small no one will see me.

I hurry toward the side door. Gino, the guard, winks at me. I'm a senior. I'm allowed out at lunch. He asks, "How's our boy?"

I freeze. He means Jimmy. He must have known too about the beaner-hopping excursions. He holds the door open for me. He tells me to "keep the faith." He definitely knows. He deals pot on the side when he's not working school security. If he knows, everybody knows. I slam out the door. Gino has never flirted with me before. I don't get it.

The school parking lot. The baseball fields. The empty gleaming bleachers. The electronic scoreboard flashes news: GAME SUNDAY AT 1 P.M. ALL ARE WELCOME. Except Jimmy.

White and blue, our school colors, dart back and forth on the endless green fields. I see Sean against the fence by the athletic fields and he sees me. I wonder what he's thinking, out on bail, young enough for juvenile court, his best friend facing what he's facing. I still can't say it. If somehow I say *murder* and *Jimmy* in the same sentence it'll be true.

Sean waves to me and throws me one of his goofy smiles—the same one that's in our first-grade class picture, except then he was missing his front tooth. The coach must have arranged an extra practice session for them, which they'll need with Jimmy out. He jogs toward me, in his shorts and a school T-shirt. It's too painful, reminding me of Jimmy, of how I loved to watch him do laps around the field. I climb into my car. At the parking lot's end, I jam the brakes too hard, jolt to a stop. I look too many times for traffic that doesn't appear. I glance back. Sean is stopped in the middle of the parking lot, looking lost. Nobody else is following me. Nobody really cares. I could go anywhere, the beach or home. Turn left, head south. I go where I have to go.

Tommy Thompson

I do what I have to do.

I work only one shift. Lookit, I may not be the brightest guy around, but I know what I've been doing. Working around the clock has been destroying my little girl. It put her in the arms of that boy.

I feel energized by my decision to get home to my daughter. We're going to go out to the diner tonight. Just her and me.

Of course, the L.I.E. is jam-packed on a Friday afternoon in June. It's one long parking lot from Queens. An hour and counting. Trucks and cars and grandmas who shouldn't be driving on the L.I.E. at any hour crowd the road.

I'm jealous of the HOV lane, of cars of husbands and wives, and other pairs. Yet even that far lane isn't going much faster than mine. Lookit, at least I'm nearing home. I sense it, more like a homing pigeon, than see it. I cut some poor bastard off. I'm sweating like a pig. I open all the windows. It's spring, isn't it? But all I can smell is my armpits, exhaust from the tractor-trailer I'm following, and stale beer from the empty cans in the backseat. What I'm smelling is the seediness of my life, its disintegration.

I smack the horn. What's slowing us down? When the traffic speeds up, I speed up faster, ride the bumper in front of me. I skid onto the shoulder and snake past cars slowing down to gawk at an accident in the westbound lanes. What are these people, idiots? Don't they realize I have to get home for my little girl?

I'm not even sure when she gets out of school. Two p.m.? Three-fifteen? She used to have a lot of after-school activities. Last year she was even on the math team that placed in the all-county finals. Not that anyone in this town cares about the math team. Lookit, I was proud of her. Her mother was even prouder.

When Skylar first started dating Jimmy, I liked him. I thought he was a decent influence on her. Brought her out of her shell and everything after her mother's passing. But that's over. Even if he beats this, he isn't coming anywhere near my daughter.

Lookit, I've made a decision. We're putting the house up for sale. We're moving out of Long Island. I'm thinking Durham, North Carolina. If she doesn't want to go to Boston College, there are plenty of good schools down there.

Not that I've ever been down there. Never got to travel much. We even liked to take our vacations out east, Montauk, but my partner at work, Charlie, says Durham's a great town. He grew up there. Charlie thinks I have to sell this old car if I'm going to move to North Carolina. He says I've got to drive a pickup truck down there, and I like that idea. Even the idea of me behind a pickup makes me sit a little higher in my beat-up four-door.

I should invite Charlie and his wife out for a barbecue before the end of the summer. He's always talking about how he loves Carolina barbecue, as if I knew the difference. Give me a Golden Arches burger, I always say, just to drive him crazy. Charlie's a good guy and an excellent paramedic.

I don't think he'd come out, though, not that I've ever asked, even when Renee suggested it. She was incredibly friendly and open, always inviting people over. I had to point out that he never invited us over to his house. At the end of the day, I had to say to her: Charlie and me work together fine, let's leave it at that. He did attend Renee's funeral. I was grateful. And lookit, his daughter, Janice, is a lawyer. He said I could go talk to her about all this trouble. It may be a good idea to have a black lawyer. I'm going to owe that guy more than I already do.

I scoot into our driveway. An hour and forty-five minutes to get home. That's a crime, but that's the L.I.E. As I scramble out of the car, I'm still thinking about this idea of selling the house, buying a pickup truck, a red one, and moving to North Carolina. This is what America is about: the chance to start new. To leave the past behind. That's America.

I've got to tell Skylar about my plan as soon as she gets home. I call for her, "Skylar! Skylar! Sky-baby!" though I know she's not home. Her car isn't here, though I like to call her name anyway. I always have. It reminds me that there are possibilities.

I stop shouting in the middle of the kitchen. Breakfast and dinner dishes, from the night before or the night before that, clutter the table. I clear them off in a clattering swoop. I'm going to clean up this whole place. Get it ready to sell.

I push open all the windows. Let's start with airing it out. How did I miss this?

Under the living room windows is a dead flower bed. Nobody remembered to plant bulbs last fall. No one went down to the Garden Center and bought trays of flowers.

My knees sink a bit. Renee and I loved to plant together even if I complained the whole time about the extra work. But enough of that. I'm all action now. We can add getting some petunias to the list. Selling a house is about curb appeal. No falling asleep in my chair with the game on tonight even if the Mets are playing the Yankees. I catch a whiff of my pits and think: Shower first, before Skylar gets home, before we start planning our new life.

Lisa Marie Murano

The word is out.

Everyone is supposed to meet up at the Dunkin' Donuts by eight p.m. It's earlier than usual and on Friday instead of Saturday. Skylar and Sean are now being asked specifically, though still voluntarily, to come down to the police station first thing on Monday morning for further questioning.

And the other thing is Jimmy. He is obviously being kept against his will. Just because his father can't make bail. I decide to ask my mother about raising funds for his bail, since she's always been the queen of fund-raising for the PTA: cookie dough sales and holiday wrapping paper. I go into her domain. Her den. All white, bright white walls, white furniture, white carpet. My mother is obsessed with the house, but especially this room. She likes to say she lives in the clouds, above it all. Kicking off my flip-flops, entering her world, I give her a quick hug. She pulls away even quicker, falling back into her white couch.

"Jimmy Seeger isn't a cause," she says, after I've made my case. "He's misguided. I wish I knew his family better. They must have issues." *Issues* is my mother's catch-all for "it's not my problem."

"If I were in jail, Mom, would you post bail?"

"If you were in jail, I'd be in my grave, so I wouldn't have to worry."

"No one in this family is posting bail for anybody!" screams my father from the upstairs bathroom.

"I won't have a conversation with you from your throne," shouts my mother. At her side is her drink, a martini, which she

135

tastes with the tip of her tongue. She's taken to drinking vodka martinis, as if they're better. "I hope this vodka isn't watered down again, angel," she says, sliding me a glance. "Oh, I know, it's convenient for us to have little white lies with one another. It keeps our lives, our town, running smoothly."

"Mom. I'm going out. To Dunkin' Donuts. With everyone else. Not a bar."

She studies me up and down.

"What happened that night?" calls out my father from the bathroom. "Where did you say you were again?" He flushes.

"I was right across the street at Skylar's," I call back.

"You were there all night?"

"Mom, do I have to be interrogated by someone on the toilet?"

"Here, try this, angel. Just a sip."

"I don't like martinis."

"How do you know if you don't try?" And my mother giggles. "I sound like I'm trying to get you to eat carrots. Oh, well. You never ate carrots either and you came out okay. Or maybe you have tried?" She sighs. "Here's to our town."

My father struts in, tucking in his pink button-down oxford. "I got to tell you—I got some news on Jimmy and his family."

My mother offers him a drink. He waves her away. She adds more olives to her glass. I'm suddenly thirsty. But I need to keep my focus until this is over. I'm swearing off any mind-altering substances until Jimmy is free.

My father grins. "You want to know about Jimmy Seeger's family. I got the goods on them from a friend of mine."

"What friend?" I ask. My father doesn't have any friends.

"A friend. In the know." And since he likes his dramatic

moments when my mother and I are paying attention to him, he makes us wait, twirling his pinky ring, pausing to pour himself a drink, only a club soda with lime. He usually likes to stay sober through dinner. Then he thrusts a bottled water at me, as if he knows I must be thirsty too.

Finally, he begins, "Okay. This friend knows them from Montauk. He knows that Jimmy has a history of causing trouble. This isn't the first time he was arrested. Apparently, the local police hauled him in about a year ago. They caught him spray-painting graffiti, ugly stuff, swastikas, on cars in certain high-class neighborhoods. His father went before the judge pleading that he was a 9/11 hero and this and that and his kid was let go. But my friend did some research on him. Seems that James Seeger, Sr., was there with the cleanup on the Wednesday after that fateful day, 9/12/2001. But he disappeared after that for over a month. His family thought that something had happened to him in connection with the disaster. It was a horrible time. Something had happened to him."

"Don't keep us in suspense," murmurs my mother, shaking her drink with a vigor she doesn't give to many other activities, except PTA fund-raising and making sure that there's an absence of color in our house.

"Get this. Sure, he disappeared. He was losing his shirt down in Atlantic City. Oh, he disappeared. Into the casinos. But he's still collecting disability based on the lie of his sacrifice. Can you believe it?"

"Some people," says my mother, her general response to anything shocking my father says. "You think you know them, or their families, but you don't know them at all."

My father turns to me. "Did you ever hear Jimmy say anything inflammatory against anybody at school?"

"Never," I reply, thinking that *beaners* can have multiple meanings.

My father bears down on me as I suck down his bottled water. "I want you to tell me again that you were with Skylar in her house all night."

"I was there. You have to believe me," I say, my voice quavering, and I really do mean it: he has to believe me. I have to be able to convince my father in order to convince others.

"I don't know what happened that night and I don't care. I only care about you. They're going to charge your friend Jimmy with murder and the only thing that is saving that idiot Mayer is that he's a minor. I don't want my family involved in this in any way going forward. You understand me? There will be no 'free Jimmy Seeger' rallies. There will be no plans to visit him or attend any hearing or any trial unless you must, and then I will go with you and make sure you say nothing." My father loves to give lectures.

"I'm just remembering something too," says my mother, like she's the teacher's pet. "She was home before midnight."

This isn't true.

"I was up. I had insomnia that night. Lisa Marie was back here and in bed."

"Let's all stay with this story. Got it?" My father glances over at my mother. She nods her head and smiles flirtatiously. He can't help it; he smirks back. They are going to be very happy when I go away to college next year.

"Where are you off to tonight?" he says, pulling back to me for a second even though they want me out of the house.

"Boring night. No one feels like having fun." This is the truth.

"This shouldn't be the way you end your junior year," says my father, softening.

My mother straightens up, the way she does when she's in the middle of drinking "just one more." "Wait a minute. Shouldn't there be some consequences here? Maybe we should talk about it more, just as a family? Have a family discussion? A young man is dead. And what do I want to say? A young man is dead. Murdered by our town."

My father shakes his head. "What are you talking about, Virginia? It didn't happen right here. It happened down by the turnpike."

My mother wipes spit or vodka from her pumped-up lips, in a gesture that signals only a short retreat. She must have been drinking all afternoon. After all, it's Friday. "Maybe you're right. It was those two brothers, apparently walking, just walking, just brothers, walking, who were uncivilized. Uncivil? How dare they think they could hitchhike to our town?"

"Ginny, come on, you're making like this is the end of the world instead of some incident with kids," says my father lightly, with an effort on my behalf to distract her. "We have no standing in this, it's not our fight. And I don't think it's the end of the world. I think we have a few more innings left. And even you said she was at the party. Your angel was home by midnight."

"Mom, you're confused. Isn't she, Dad?"

My mother swoops off her couch. "Don't lie to me. Lie to everyone else, angel. But don't lie to me. Now tell me. One last time. Did you have anything to do with that young man's death? Anything at all?"

"No."

"No?" my mother parrots me, inches from me, swaying. Now she's focusing on me, but I'm finished. That's all I'm saying when I realize she doesn't have a rebuke, a plan of what to do next. I've won.

"No is no," my father erupts with. "What choice do we have, Ginny, but to believe in our daughter?" He sighs, bending, groping in the liquor cabinet. Lucky for her and me, he opens a new bottle of vodka and begins fixing a martini. "It's not our fight, Ginny," he repeats.

My mother squeezes her arms around my father's waist. He kisses her neck. She buries her face in the pink of his oxford.

Get me out of here.

Running out of my house, I see Mr. Thompson on his knees. He's digging in the dirt near the house. The whole lawn is rutted and dead. He's using a spoon or his hands. He looks like a mutt scratching at the dirt with front paws. His back is to me, so I don't have to wave hello.

I do wonder where Skylar is. Her car is nowhere to be seen. Maybe she's already on her way over to Dunkin' Donuts, but usually she waits for me and her car follows mine. We could share one car or we could even walk, but no one does that.

Now Mr. Thompson's lying in the dirt. Facedown. But moving.

I need my friends.

At Dunkin' Donuts we're spreading out along the back of the parking lot. The trees throw shadows over our cars like a blanket.

We crowd close to one another, nobody speaking much. Everybody is here except for Skylar. She cut out early from school. I know she is avoiding me. I call her. I text her. No Skylar.

Like always, Benny totes out doughnuts for everybody. This time he remembers Sean's favorite, chocolate with chocolate frosting and sprinkles, same as when he was a kid. Sean digs his fingers into the box before Benny can even put them down on the roof of one of the cars. He smears his face with chocolate, goofing around. Howls at the moon. Everyone laughs, except me. He paws at my arm, yips at my ear, trying to make me laugh too. I'm not laughing.

"What the hell is wrong with you? Are you high?" I hiss, backing away from him into the shadows, hating how the darkness falls around me from the trees.

"No."

"What's wrong?"

"How about you and me in the Camaro?"

"Do you need a ride somewhere?" I ask, pretending not to know that he's wanting something else that I'm not going to do. Anyway, it's so pathetic that he won't drive these days. I mean, I know, it was what every psychologist on TV calls a traumatic experience. Maybe I'll give him a ride tonight, but that's all. He's no Jimmy. No BJ. "Can you tell me what is wrong, Sean?"

"Everything is just wonderful, isn't it, Lisa Marie?"

"Clean off your face. We all have a lot to talk about. This isn't all about you, Sean."

"Who is it about? Is it about you? Or is it about all of us?" he says, with a dumb look on his greased-up face.

"Do you want to go home? Would that help?"

He drags the back of his hand across his lips like a little kid.

"What more can I do for you, Sean? If you had somewhere to go, I'd let you borrow my car, even though my father doesn't like me to do that," I say, squeezing in a small lie. Nobody drives Lisa Marie's Camaro but Lisa Marie.

"I don't have anywhere I need to be," he mumbles, sulking off toward Jake Kroll and the others.

Thing is, Sean should have been smarter that night. He should have kept himself—and Jimmy—to the plan. Bean them, throw an old baseball or a rock, scare them off, get them running. I've been turning it all over in my head. Jimmy's idea of beaner-hopping, a weekly activity at most, not something that happened every day. It wasn't worse than some other things that went on around here. All Sean wanted to do was get drunk, get high, hang out with Jimmy. I mean, I know something went wrong that night. I'm not clueless.

I walk back over to him with the box of doughnuts as an offering. "Maybe you should eat a doughnut?"

He says he's lost his taste for doughnuts. He's such a bad liar. They remind him of Jimmy. Me too.

"Maybe just one will make you feel better?"

"Can't you see this is eating me alive, Lisa Marie?" He tries now to smack the chocolate off his face, and it's worse, grimy, mixed with spit or tears.

"Let's all talk," I say in a low voice, wishing he could straighten up; he's all slouched over. "That's the only way we're all going to figure out what to do and how to help each other."

He stares at me like I don't know what I'm talking about. But if Jimmy were here we'd have a plan. Everything we did together was more exciting with him. He'd call it his "plan of action." I loved how Jimmy was so decisive.

I look at us all. Almost everyone is here, except for Skylar. We're all facing west, watching the last of the light leave us. We're sitting on our cars or lounging against bumpers and we're feeling our loss, a sense that it's the end of things. Finally, I say to all, "We have to do something. Something to support Jimmy and everyone else. Something at the baseball game on Sunday."

Everyone shifts toward me to listen more, except for Sean. Sean steps out from the shadows, shouting, "What?" at me. "What the hell are you thinking?"

I face him full-on. "Sean," I say with extra reasonableness because he has had such a wrong attitude all night, and I think I can reach him with this, "I've been thinking of this a lot—is what happened so different from that extreme fighting you like so much? Or making sure that those kids from the garden apartments weren't kicking around their ball on our soccer fields?"

"I was twelve. We pushed them down. They pushed us. We stuck their ball with Kroll's Boy Scout knife. That was different."

"Was it? I don't think so."

"It was. Different." Jimmy would never talk to me, or anybody, like that. "Those two brothers weren't agreeing to fight. It wasn't a matchup. It wasn't like that at all. I don't know what it was. Don't listen to me. I don't know anything—"

"Shut up. Sean, if you think about it my way, maybe it would help you. You aren't thinking about it the right way."

He turns away from me, when I am only trying to comfort him. I can't believe him. He is so frustrating. "I think we should focus on Sunday and what we can do for Jimmy there," I say to everyone.

A voice in the shadows pipes up. "The school isn't going to let us do anything. This isn't a rally for a kid with cancer. We know what Jimmy and everybody else was doing, don't we?" says Jake, who has nothing but this to share tonight.

Someone shouts out, "Just jealous you weren't in on it, Kroll."

"I was on Jimmy's list," Jake snaps back. "But I'm just wondering, isn't anybody wondering, why none of us thought twice?"

"No," the voice says with a laugh, and others join in. "You're the only one who's confused." More laughter gallops through the shadows. And the entire baseball team, all except Sean, chuck Jake into the Dumpster, shouting, "Coward," and jostling his legs up and into the garbage of stale doughnuts and half-drunk coffees.

I have to focus everyone back on me, though the sight of Jake Kroll climbing out of the garbage is hilarious. "Not official," I continue with urgency. "Something only we know that we're doing for him during the baseball game. Unrolling a banner, maybe a flag, with his name on it? Something meaningful. Something that shows our true team spirit. Nothing disrespectful. Maybe we chant 'Jimmy' instead of cheering when anyone gets out on the other team? That could be fun. Anyway, what we need is a plan of action."

A buzz rises in the crowd. Everybody likes having a plan of action. Now Skylar shows up.

Tommy Thompson

So I'm planting petunias.

I went to the garden center and the place stunk like shit like always, and I bought a wagonful of petunias. I tried to remember the other kinds we liked. I couldn't.

I thought Skylar would be home by now to stick them in the ground with me. I'm kneeling here in front of the house digging. I haven't even taken the flowers out of the car yet. They're waiting in the backseat like children. I even left the window open for them.

I'm actually more lying in the dirt. Face down. I've given up with the trenches. I couldn't find any of Renee's garden tools. I was clawing at the ground with my hands, because I couldn't find the right tool. When Renee gardened, she always wore special gloves for her hands. After she died, I boxed up a lot of her things and stuffed them in one of those rental storage units. I thought it would help Skylar—and me. The tools are probably there.

A fresh root smell braces me. Shoots push up. Maybe some grass or a bulb sprung to life. I should water. Dirt blooms around my head.

I flip over on my back. The disturbed ground is soft under my head. I'll finish planting in the morning. Maybe Skylar will help.

I look up and thank her for our daughter. I say her name. I always do. *Renee.*

James Seeger, Sr.
Jimmy's dad

This is killing me—seeing Jimmy in jail and not having the money for bail. But we've never been like other families, I tell Jimmy. We're special. We know who we are. But it's killing me to see him there. Killing me.

I'm in the basement, on my knees, on this shitty brown carpet stinking of mildew and rot, in front of this broken-down fireplace, fixing things. My wife knew enough to leave me alone. All day she was begging me to ask her mother for the bail money. She said that's the only way her tight-assed mother would relent. Always thought she was better than me. Always reminding me that her family was just a couple of boats behind the *Mayflower*. I wasn't going to ask her for money at all. But I did. My mother-in-law hates my guts—called me a phony as she handed me the money for the lawyer for her grandson. Only the lawyer. No way was she putting up her property for the bond. It's been in her family too long to risk it on her only grandson. Idiot. No way, I can't ask that woman for anything more.

I've got to do the dirty work. I always do. But I'd do anything for my kid. Anything. I rented a wood chipper from the hardware store. I didn't tell the moron behind the counter what it was for. If anybody asked, I was going to say flower beds. That moron held me up, though, asking for two kinds of ID and a deposit, moving in slow motion behind the counter. By the time I got the wood chipper, I was so angry I could have beat his brains out. But I had a job to do.

The bat, Jimmy's good bat, the top-of-the-line Louisville Slugger, the one I bought for him to hit home runs with, was right where I had buried it in the backyard after fishin' it out of that Dumpster. It was covered with blood and strands of hair and even a piece of scalp, I think. What a waste.

Anyway, do you think that Coach Martinez was going to let my son hit cleanup?

What does it matter now? The entire major league is made up of players who only speak Spanish or Japanese. Jimmy never had a chance.

One thing I am glad for is that he didn't use a metal bat. What would I have done with that?

I cut up this beautiful piece of wood into a million pieces and gather them all with extreme care and burn them in the fireplace. I scrape the ashes out. All winter long my wife harped on me about building a fire, and here it is and she's in church on her knees praying. Lucky for me, she brought our youngest son. Damn kid goes everywhere with her. Mama's boy. I got to change that.

I hold the ashes in a dustbin and slide them into the toilet, flush. I'm on my knees on this crappy pink-and-green tile like I'm sick or drunk. I'm neither. My heart hurts. My son is behind bars, for what?

For fighting for America.

He's getting the short end of the stick on this.

So the brother might be able to place him there, that night. He's their eyewitness, a seventeen-year-old Mexican dropout. Our lawyer's found out that the brother had a fake Social Security number on him. He's a rat. A scab. Aiming to get the jobs of hardworking Americans like me.

Flush again. Wipe around the bowl.

And the drugs. Don't forget about the drugs. This is the best part. The lawyer said two bags of pot were found in his gym bag. He was no angel either. Probably some kind of gang member into who knows what.

It's killing me. That Mexican died. Why the hell did he have to die? Now they want to charge my boy with murder and hate crimes. My son says that he didn't kill that damn Mexican. I don't care if he says he's from El Salvador—same thing—Jimmy didn't kill anybody. Maybe it was the other boy, that goofball Sean Mayer with his I'm-the-head-of-the-Board-of-Education fat-ass mother and sissy-girl father. Jimmy didn't kill nobody. And don't get me started about hate crimes. What the hell is that? We're supposed to love everybody? Get real. Maybe my son chased them. But haven't these people literally overrun our country? Jimmy didn't kill. Not my son. Maybe Jimmy had to hit him. Once. Maybe those two brothers were bothering him.

My son didn't kill anybody. Not the boy I raised to hit over .400.

It was self-defense. Maybe one of those guys had a gun. They were hitchhiking, weren't they? What kinds of people hitchhike these days? Around here, only those kind. It was self-defense, that's the good word from the lawyer today.

My son was defending himself—and Sean, and our country, I'd add. They should be giving him a medal.

Flush again.

Guns. Drugs. Gangs. They do what they please. Sneak across the border, practically invade our country. No one stops them. Isn't the main job of government to protect its people? This is what happens when Americans have to take justice into their own hands.

I straighten up. Flush again for good measure. Maybe I should go down to Atlantic City. I'm due some luck.

At least Jimmy was smart enough to hide the bat in that Dumpster behind the Dunkin' Donuts and to tell me exactly where to find it. I'd do anything for my kid. Anything. Even climb into a stinkin' Dumpster.

But I've got to admit. I'm worried. Jimmy said he saw his little girlfriend following him that night. I know why he likes that girl, Skylar. She's like his mother. She's book smart, not street smart. Too needy, I said to him after I met her, wearing all black, like some punk, and hanging behind my son. Granted, there's some appeal there. Those green eyes. And those legs, like a stork. Can't fly away. But if I was him I would have jumped on the friend, the one in the hot pink.

Jimmy is strong. He'll be okay in that county jail. The one thing I told him was to keep on sweet-talking that girlfriend of his. I almost wish he had knocked her up. A girl with a kid is never going to give up the father.

But he tells me that she's with the program. Jimmy is also sure that Sean is—scared to death not to be. If not, they all hang together. Not literally, of course. No one hangs anymore. I want to make sure my son gets justice, that's all.

I show up. Maybe it's out of habit. Lisa Marie calls or texts and I come.

Everyone I've been avoiding the past two days surrounds me in the Dunkin' Donuts parking lot. They think I've seen Jimmy, but I quickly tell them it's happening on Saturday, that I can't wait, that I'm going to be there as early as I can, that I'm going even though my father is going to kill me for it. Those aren't his words, he never says "kill," but everyone knows what I mean and the point is I am seeing Jimmy. They press toward me. An open hand strokes my back. Everyone understands that this is hard, that I'm doing all I can to stand by Jimmy, that it's unfair, that all of us are being singled out for something, we don't know what—who we are, maybe, and that should bind us together even more, and it does to the point I'm starting to suffocate. I don't even know why I'm here.

Lisa Marie sees something is wrong. "Why so quiet? What happened to my friend that couldn't shut up for months about Jimmy?"

I shrug. I count the number of cars. I group people in twos and then threes. I decide I like odds better and group in fives. Everyone is looking at me, waiting for me to say something. "I'm just thinking of seeing him, that's all."

Lisa Marie hugs me. "Where have you been?"

"Nowhere." I don't dare to tell anyone, including Lisa Marie, about going back there again, to no-man's-land, about seeing Carlos Cortez again. About jumping out of my Mustang and rushing across the parking lot to him and asking his forgiveness and— I didn't do that. I mean, I wanted to. I was there, again. And so was he. And—

"We were all worried about you, Skylar," Lisa Marie is saying. "Don't do that again! Go off for hours. Now tell me, where'd you go?"

Stale doughnuts shine in a box. I stuff one in my mouth. I haven't eaten anything all day. Chocolate. I gag. "I think I should go. Home."

"Should we let Skylar go?" says Lisa Marie to the crowd. "We have to let her in on our plans for Sunday." There are hoots and no's and yes's and a rearranging of my groupings as they shift in the darkness.

"What plans?" I had been thinking of going to this prayer vigil tomorrow morning. I heard it announced on the car radio. I was thinking that it would be a nice thing to do, maybe the right thing to do. Not that I am into prayer, not that I ever attend church, except for midnight mass on Christmas Eve because everyone goes. Some, like Sean, went stoned last year. Not that anyone would go with me if I asked. I'm sure Lisa Marie would advise against it. I probably won't go.

"I think you should go home now and we'll talk in the morning. But I don't think you should go home alone. Sean, why don't you ride home with Skylar since you don't have your car?" This is Lisa Marie taking charge of my life, again.

"You don't have your car?" I ask Sean.

Sean shoots me his biggest, goofiest of smiles. "My father won't let me use it after 'the incident.'"

"Okay," I say to Sean. "But I'm exhausted. I have to go now."

Lisa Marie blocks my way to the car. Pinching my arm, she guides me into the shadows, far from our cars, our crowd. I want to run.

"I just want to make sure again, for like the thousandth time, that you and me are together on this. I was at your house last Saturday night, right?"

This is Lisa Marie, who obsessed over her prom dress, over the limousine, over the post-party beach party. I hope no one expects me still to go to any of it.

"Right, Skylar?"

I nod my head. This is true, sort of. All four of us—me, Lisa Marie, Sean, and Jimmy—went there after Dunkin' Donuts. Jimmy and Sean followed us back to my house. Nobody went inside except me, for a second, grabbing beers for Jimmy and Sean. Jimmy leaned against the Mustang in the driveway, in the light of a full moon, looking—oh, God, even now I can see him—his long legs, his arms crossed over his chest, his blue eyes dark, angry at something, anything—impatient, maybe that's it. Lisa Marie and Sean hung out on the front steps, knee to knee, killing time, waiting for Jimmy to be ready to go. Jimmy alternated kissing me, hungry kisses, and finishing off one of my father's beers, then another and—

"Jimmy and Sean left us there."

I am dumb. Yes. That is true.

"But we don't know where they went, correct? Maybe they went to get some ice cream or here for doughnuts or for a ride. Thing is, we don't know where in the world they could have gone, do we? Please answer me, Skylar. This is what I am going to say. You can't say anything different to anyone."

I close my eyes. I am blind. I open them and she is still there, closer than before, a second ago.

"Focus, Skylar. Our plan was to wait for them, but it got late and I went home. I walked back across the street. My mother thinks it was midnight. She remembers the time. She remembers what she was watching on television when I walked into the house."

That night. Last Saturday night. At around midnight we were driving behind Sean's SUV, far enough behind that they couldn't spot us. They were racing through yellow lights. I drove like an old lady out too late. But Lisa Marie and I were giggling, screeching if we lost them for a second. We had vodka and no-calorie lemonade in a water bottle between us, Lisa Marie's drink on the go. We joked about being the first girls out on a beaner-hopping field maneuver. We laughed the whole way. We wanted to be there. I chose Jimmy or he chose me, but that doesn't matter. That night I didn't think anything of following him. I would have gone anywhere.

Next to me, sunk in the seat, with her window wide open, Lisa Marie drank. I was good about never drinking and driving. But truth be told, I had had some earlier and was buzzing and feeling good. Or, as Lisa Marie would say, I was feeling no pain.

Jimmy and Sean stopped as if they were going to pick up two hitchhikers. I pulled into the far side of the restaurant behind a Dumpster. So we could surprise them. In less than a minute, Lisa Marie passed out, with the water bottle drooping from her lips.

I watched Sean and Jimmy, really only Jimmy. It excited me even more than being with them. Their profiles were clear in the moonlight. Each one had a hand gripping the top of the SUV. It was like they were two sides of one guy—

"Isn't that what happened, Skylar? I went home."

I am mute.

"Isn't this the truth, Skylar? You have to say it and believe it. I'm saying it, so it must be true, correct?"

I am dumb and mute and in a moment will go blind.

"So we're together on this, correct?"

My head nods because it has always been easier to agree with Lisa Marie.

"So Sean, are you going to go with Skylar?"

I don't think he will. He certainly can see that I'm in no condition to drive, that I can't move, that I have become stone. But tonight, he shrugs and follows me into the car, sliding into the passenger seat, buckling himself in.

"Let's go," he says. "Let's get far away from here."

"Where are we going?" Skylar asks, creeping the car forward toward the street. She looks left and right and left and right again.

"Just go."

"Where?"

This has always been Skylar's problem. She is without the imagination needed to imagine the unimaginable. Everything is on face value for her. That's what Jimmy said—and he liked to dissect her and everyone else.

"Just go," I say abruptly, wanting more than anything else to shake my thoughts free of Jimmy.

"Home?"

"Anywhere but home," and I add in the old Sean voice, "Hey, it's not even ten p.m. Our parents don't need to know where their children are."

She doesn't laugh. At least she used to laugh with me, didn't she? I've known Skylar my whole life. She was always the girl next door, an only child, loving my house stuffed with my sisters and me. I wanted out and she wanted in.

Now she's gripping the wheel like I'm going to snatch it from her. She's pulling out of the parking lot as slow as my grandma.

"Come on," I urge, "let's go."

"Are you high? I don't feel like being with you when you're high. I don't feel like dealing with any more craziness."

"I'm stone—"

"I'm going home."

"Skylar, hey. Let me talk for once. I'm stone-cold sober, okay?"

She gives me that look that says she doesn't believe me, she shouldn't believe me, she should know better than to believe me. I don't know how I'll ever convince anyone I'm telling the truth.

"Go east," I shout as we near the L.I.E. "East. East. East. To the end. East, Skylar!"

I'm jumping up and down in the seat. I am grabbing the wheel. She's stronger than I thought. She's pulling back. We skid off the road.

I let go. I don't want her to crash us into a tree.

"East?" she asks, banging over the grass and shoulder and back to the road.

"A little trip," I say, easing back in the seat, wanting to pump the radio up, wanting to blast it and— Stop! Stop! Stop! You promised. You told your father you'd come clean. You'd tell the truth. You'd do the deal. You'd be the traitor, the turncoat, the rat—

"You ever think of that night?" she asks.

"What night?" As if there are any others.

But she surprises me. "The night we stayed up until midnight on the swing in your backyard."

What is she talking about?

"The tire, Sean. The first night after your father hung the tire in the backyard. We thought we could make a record, spend the night swinging in the tire. It was the middle of summer. I guess we were eight or nine. Fireflies surrounded us. I think your mother forgot that we were out there or she was inside having a drink with my mother. Lemonade. Your mother liked to make real lemonade and my mother loved to drink it. She asked for it in the end."

I stretch way back in the seat. "We didn't care that they forgot us on the tire."

"They were always there, our parents, until they weren't. At least mine. I can't lose someone else in my life, you understand that, don't you, Sean?"

She doesn't say anything else and I'm thinking about how I loved that tire, how I begged for it, how I had to have it that summer more than going to the pool or bowling or day camp or anything else. My mother wanted a play set for me: a wood fort and yellow plastic swings. Something that cost a small fortune, she said, as if that would persuade me. But I wanted a rope and a tire off my tree. That's all I wanted, that's all I want.

I sit straight up. "If I tell what happened, I go free, no charges, no record, no nothing. I go off to college, have a life."

"What about Jimmy?"

"Stay in your lane, okay? Do you want me to drive?" Though I actually haven't been behind the wheel since that night. And I don't want to drive. It isn't because my father didn't want me to have the car that I haven't been driving. I can't get behind the wheel. I shake. I have double vision. Now I need Skylar to drive. There are hardly any cars on the road. Out here, the L.I.E. is a straight road. Each car seems to take its own lane as if by some agreement. The moon looks pressed into the sky, a sliver rising in front of us. Wasn't it a full moon that night? Why do I remember being bathed in light?

"You guys weren't there alone." Skylar steps on the gas as if to pass someone, but all she does is speed up and keep going with a fierce determination set on her face. When she was young, and I was young, she'd push me on that tire swing with the same look before demanding that I do the same for her.

"I know you and Lisa Marie were following us."

"Did you see us?"

"I did. And Lisa Marie told me you followed us," I admit. "But she said that she was out cold."

"She *was* out cold."

"But you weren't?" I glance over at her. She's at least holding the wheel with both hands, and they are delicate, bloodless hands, nails bitten down to the skin.

"I wish I was."

"That would never be you."

"Who am I, Sean?"

"Don't ask me," I say. "I don't know who any of us are anymore."

She won't look at me. Five or ten minutes must pass; time expands along the inky black road. As if in a middle of a thought, she asks, "Jimmy didn't see us? Lisa Marie and me?"

He zeroed in on the two brothers, calling them fags and homos to start. He barely knew I was there. "Jimmy never told me he saw your car," is all I say.

"And the knife? Mr. Seeger said they had a knife?"

"A knife? I don't know. I don't think so. What are you saying?"

"I don't know."

"And don't ask me," I say in a low, detached voice, "about the bat. After it was over, I never saw that bat again."

"I wasn't going to." Her thin shoulders sink into her spare self. It's like she's backup Skylar these days. The bigger, robust, confident Skylar of tire swings and all-night talks went on the disabled list and never returned after her mother died.

"So you didn't see everything that happened?" I ask gently.

"Enough. I don't know. No. I drove off. It was crazy."

"You don't know. How crazy."

One day I woke up before dawn and swung in the tire in my cowboy pajamas. The grass was still wet, the tire damp. The birds greeted me, surprised, perching on the branches above my head as if to announce my arrival, and I swung there until breakfast and would have stayed out there all morning if my mother hadn't tempted me into the house with doughnuts and lemonade.

"What was crazy? Tell me, Sean." She whispers, as if there are other people in the car with us.

"I don't know, Skylar," I start out, staring out the window, feeling as if I'm floating in darkness, feeling as if it's safer to talk. "It was just supposed to be us out beaning Mexicans. Wasn't anything. Wasn't nothing. Like killing invaders or aliens—nobody thought differently—it was only us out on patrol, on a maneuver." I'm using the Jimmy talk again. It was my whole life the last year. It was what we talked about when we were avoiding talking about the prom because that's what the girls talked about. It was our inside joke and a sick one. I'm not a psychopath. I know it was sick, but it was Jimmy and with him it wasn't.

"Nobody did, Sean."

"Isn't that weird in a way? Shouldn't someone have said something?"

Gnawing her bottom lip, she draws blood.

"Nobody did," I finally agree. "We can't blame ourselves. That's what my father says." Jimmy made us think we were doing something right. That was the genius of Jimmy. That's what was sick about it. He thought he was being some kind of hero. And still, nobody has told me what I did was wrong. I don't think my parents want to lecture me, they think I'm going through enough. My father says if I tell the prosecutors what I need to tell them to get off, I'll be able to put this behind me.

I'm never going to be able to put this behind me. I'm never going to be able to move on. I did something that led to another person's death. "Who is to blame, then?" I ask Skylar the question I should have asked my father.

"I don't know," she says, because she won't say Jimmy. Or me. Or anybody. None of us are to blame. He beat himself to death.

"So is everyone going to hate me for talking?" I say, cutting into my own thoughts, wishing I was stoned, wishing I was flat on my back, or better yet, in my tire swing, stoned, plugged in to the crickets and stars and sky.

"I won't."

I stop her from saying more. "I don't think Lisa Marie will ever talk to me again." And I add with a forced smile, "Maybe that's a good thing?"

She clutches the wheel, studying the L.I.E. as if more cars will appear, or hitchhikers or ghosts. "Let's not talk about Lisa Marie."

"Remember the Fourth of July fair?" I ask.

"I wasn't there this year. My mom—"

"Oh, yeah. Jimmy's father was at the fair. He was being honored. He's one of those 9/11 heroes. My mother was up there too getting an award for doing whatever she does."

"I wasn't there," Skylar repeats.

"Jimmy was there. He saw me in my football jersey and said he was trying out for the team. He made a joke about whether he had to know how to speak Spanish with Coach Martinez. I laughed. All I cared about before Jimmy was that Martinez had played with the Mets. I didn't think of anything else. I didn't think at all."

"My mother died on the Fourth of July. That night."

"That's right," I say, touching her skinny arm, realizing I am only bringing more sadness into the world.

"You know what you don't know, Sean? What nobody knows? My father was there too."

"Where?"

"At the Towers."

I had to think for a second. That's right. Skylar's father works EMT for the city. What did Jimmy's father do again on 9/11? All I know is that his father hovered around the football and baseball fields during practice driving the coach crazy.

I glance over at her. Her lips are chapped, reminding me of when we were six or seven and would gobble down Italian ices, only cherry, our favorite, our mouths and fingers stained red, bloody red. Back then, she didn't talk a lot; she laughed a lot instead. We rode to the stars on tire swings, gobbled cherry ices, and drank fresh-made lemonade.

Now she's talking at me. "My father didn't come home. He slept down there until October, I'm sure. I was only a kid, but I remember how my mother wanted him home, how she'd dial his cell over and over trying to reach him, how everyone was afraid of more attacks. And when he came home, he smelled like burnt plastic, his face was ashen-gray, he looked older and slept forever. He never speaks about it, though."

"Why didn't I know this?" I can't even picture her dad these days. But I know he's definitely not hero material.

"He says he was just doing his job."

"That's cool," I say, because it is.

"You know I love him."

"Your dad?"

"Jimmy. But how can I love him?"

I don't have an answer for this. Even more, I don't know why I'm thinking about what it would be like to kiss her, maybe just to make her chapped lips feel better. Instead, I rub my sore neck.

"Sean?"

"I don't know," I say, quickly, and add with a laugh, "how would I know about stuff like that?"

She bites her bottom lip. "I love him."

I nod my head. "Drive faster."

Skylar stuns me. She drives even faster.

I slam my fist against the side of my head.

Neither of us says anything.

"How fast can this car go?" I finally ask her.

"I don't know."

"Let's see. Seventy-five. Eighty. Eighty-five," I count off, and she joins in, echoing me, "Seventy-five, eighty. Ninety." My father once joked that I should try out for the math team with her. I told him I didn't have time for anything else. Now I wish I had, even though I sucked at math.

"Eighty-five, ninety, is this fast enough, Sean?"

The L.I.E. streaks by. I open the window and whiff sea salt and grasses and exhaust.

"Don't stop," I yell, sticking my head out the window, screaming at no one this clear night. Or maybe I'm screaming at the moon, at Jimmy, or at me. The wind, full of sea, tears my eyes.

And then there are signs to Montauk and the end of the L.I.E. I forget the highway ends out here, that we are on something finite, not infinite, that we live on an island.

"Faster!" I scream.

Skylar obliges me. "Ninety-five, a hundred. The wheel is rattling, Sean! Look! The L.I.E. ends—up ahead, eight hundred feet. What should we do? Drive out to Montauk?"

Montauk. The end. That's what the bumper stickers say.

I pull myself back in the car.

"I don't think I can make it to Montauk," she shouts over at me.

"Me neither," I toss back at the top of my lungs.

"You have the game Sunday?"

"I have the game. You think they'd have kicked me off the team." In my life there's always been a game: soccer, Little League, floor hockey, basketball, football, baseball, what am I missing? I was always on a team—never swimming, tennis, or track. I don't know why.

"Do you think we're going to win?"

"I can't go to jail, Skylar. I can't."

"I mean the game, Sean."

"I don't care if we win." I've never said this aloud. Jimmy would hate to hear me say that. My father would hate to hear it too; he always says that even when no one is keeping score they really are. I don't know how I'll even be able to pick up a bat on Sunday.

"When are you going to talk?" She has to shout this at me. The car is shaking, the wind, a sea wind, is whipping across the car, and if she didn't shout, I would have pretended not to hear. I don't want to think about this anymore. I can't.

Finally, I say, "I think they want me to talk before the hearing next Wednesday. I think it's on Wednesday. I don't know. My father's handling it all."

"Is this what we should be doing, Sean?"

I can't tell her I'm doing it because I'm a coward. I can't bear to have my father or mother go through this. I can't bear living with myself and the sound of the bat crashing on that Mexican, that guy from El Salvador . . . that El Salvadorian? I'm a coward. That's why I'm talking, nothing more. I don't care about doing the right thing because I've already done the wrong thing. I'm a loser. There are winners and losers, and I've lost.

"Why did we do it, Sean?"

"I fucked up." I don't think she hears me. She's concentrating on driving at ninety miles plus per hour, and I can't repeat it out loud, only to myself, over and over until Skylar says she has to slow down or we'll crash at the end of the L.I.E. She tells me this evenly, in her very level-headed way. My father is always saying that Skylar is the most sensible girl he's ever met and why didn't I think of going out with her before Jimmy snatched her up? That's how my father talks. Like Skylar was a ball I dropped. But he's right. I screwed that up too.

"Sean? What should we do?"

"Go for it," I insist. Isn't that what Jimmy said last Saturday night—let's go for it? We stopped the car alongside these two guys. Who knew they were brothers?

And we were playing with them like always—until we weren't. I'm not sure what one said to Jimmy. I was in the driver's seat, even though I was way too messed up to drive. And then we were out of the car. *Let's go for it. Let's go.*

At the last possible moment, when there is still time to avert disaster, when there is time to decide to live and not die, Skylar slacks off the gas, swings right, off the L.I.E. We're on another highway but different. Pines tower. We can't see the way back. In front of us, two lanes stripe down to blackness. The moon's fled.

I close my window. She follows with hers. In the sudden quiet, my heart beats, scarred, broken, scared. *Let's go. Let's go.*

I don't know what happened next. I don't know why he had a bat in my car, except I drove Jimmy everywhere and had a lot of his stuff in my car: his history textbook that he said he never read (even though he got Scholar-Athlete of the Year with me), his dirty gym shorts, his water bottle. *Let's go. Let's go.* Why didn't I tell him to stop? Because I didn't want to stop, because we were only hopping the beaners, because I was too messed up, because somewhere along the way I had stopped thinking. *Let's go. Let's go.*

No more. Please. No more. Think of the tire swing. Swirled on that swing. Clutched the scratchy woven-hemp rope that knotted around the rubber like a lifeline. Twirled in circles until the ground spun independent of me. Staggered off, drunk on being eight or nine.

I don't know what I'm ready to do except drink more beer. I'm hopeless. I want to be eight or nine, and if I can't be that I want to be so out of it I can't see straight. I can't think straight now. I want to go somewhere, a discount mart, and pay someone to run in and buy me at least two six-packs. They run fast enough when it's for beer, Jimmy always said. I hate myself for thinking this. I smash my fist against the side of her car.

"Are you okay, Sean?"

"Drive. Don't ask me if I'm okay. I don't have an answer. How can I be okay? I'm an idiot. A moron. Jimmy said we should have killed the other brother too. Maybe he was right. I fucked up everything."

"You don't mean that?" she whispers, one translucent hand going to her pale throat. "Jimmy didn't say that?"

I feel like everything is falling away. I lose Jimmy and my friends and my life if I talk, or I go to jail and lose Jimmy and my friends and my life. Either way, I'm in last place. But it's more than that, I'm really no place.

"What about you? You're going to go along with Lisa Marie." And I want to add *like you always do,* but I don't. I have nothing left in me. I hold my breath. I want my heart to stop punching against my chest. I twist in my seat, looking straight at her, breathing as if against my will. "You don't have to say anything. Not now. Maybe if there's a trial. I mean, I'm not a lawyer, but I think that's it. I don't know. Don't listen to me, Skylar."

"I can't talk. You don't expect me to talk, do you? I'll feel like I've lost everything if I do—"

"I think we're at the point where we all have to make our own decisions, aren't we?"

"When did we get to this point?" she asks, easing up on the gas, not expecting an answer.

I give one anyway. "For me, there's nowhere to turn and nothing left to turn to. All those games we played. I thought they were life, my life, and they weren't."

"Sean—"

"No more fields. Nothing. It's over, and maybe it all didn't mean a thing, and that's the worst part. With one swing of the bat, it's all over."

"Are you okay, Sean?" she says, strained, distanced. "You have practice tomorrow? I'm seeing Jimmy—"

"Tell him for me—"

Skylar looks at me full-on with her wide sea-green eyes, and away. No matter what I do, she'll think like everyone, like Lisa Marie, like the coach and my father and Jimmy and everyone else, that I'm a loser, a hopeless loser. With one swing, it's all over.

"Tell me, Sean."

"Nothing," I say. "Staying strong."

The Mustang dives left through the trees, shoots through a short turnaround. We're not going to Montauk, the end of the end. I close my eyes. We're on the tire swing together. Skylar is counting. She wants to see how far she can count. She doesn't know then that even though numbers are infinite, we are not.

Sean hung himself.

I found him. He was hanging from a rope in the backyard early on Saturday morning. I found him first. I found him because I couldn't sleep. I thought I could, in the early morning quiet, prune back the rosebushes, spread some fertilizer my father bought, not the organic kind, pure chemicals. I was in sweats and flip-flops. There was the lightest of breezes. I wasn't sure of what I was seeing across the hedge, the bottom of Sean's legs and his muddy sneakers. I ran over with the pruning clippers in my hand and dropped them, calling out his name as if he would meet me halfway.

Sean had loosened off the tire. He had made a noose. Apparently he had jumped off the high branch with the rope around his neck. His father saw him too. He had been on his way to get bagels. He ran out as I was wrapping my arms around his son's body as if I could lift him, save him.

Sean's dad was always the dad who pulled out the fireworks on the Fourth of July—bottle rockets for the older boys and sparklers for the rest of us. He liked to organize the summer block party. He coached soccer and Little League and was even the Scout leader when Sean was into Scouting for a while. When Sean was ten or so, his dad brought home a unicycle. No one else had one. But Sean didn't want to be different, so he refused to ride it, sticking with his bright blue Schwinn. Instead, his dad rode the unicycle in every town parade, waving to Sean and his four older sisters. My parents always said the Mayers were determined to have a boy even if they had to have a dozen girls first; they succeeded after four girls. Sean was named after his father, but he wasn't a "Jr." since his mother gave him her maiden name for his middle name. I was probably the only person besides the family who knew it. Sean was their prince, an easy-going, gently goofy, always go-along-with-the-crowd prince. But for them, he could do no wrong. *He could do no wrong. Now, or ever again.* I wouldn't let him go.

Sean's dad wouldn't let Sean go either.

My father barreled through the bushes in his striped pajamas. The front of his shirt was wet, splattered with coffee.

"Sean? Sean. Step away. Let me in."

"He's dead," I screamed, as if my father didn't know.

"Stand back, toots. Please. Don't look at this. Look at me. At the sky. At anything else," he said.

"Sean? Come on, man," said my father. Placing his hands on Mr. Mayer's shoulders. "Let me handle this."

What does he want for Sean to do? I thought irrationally, crying.

"Sean, no. No, buddy," said my father, steadily to Mr. Mayer. I screamed. Mr. Mayer was clutching his son's waist, trying to lift him up, out of the homemade noose, heaving, wrenching, shouting, "Sean."

And there was my father, pulling Mr. Mayer away, disengaging father from son, and easing Sean out of the noose. I sank to my knees. I was cold and alone, wrapping my arms around myself, crying. Sean's father beat my father's back; his mother screamed from somewhere in the house; and Sean was laid by my father on the grass. My father checked Sean's pulse, shook his head, and held me in his gaze before turning and facing Mr. Mayer's fists. But instead of fighting, my father bound his arms around Mr. Mayer. He let Sean's father wail into the wall of his chest.

In a moment, or so it seemed after I found Sean's body, a swath of red lights and cries and neighbors lined around the Mayers' house. It was like a block party, though most everyone was in their pajamas.

Mr. Mayer bellowed Sean's name like Sean was lost, or, worse, like he was gone forever, and he was. Mrs. Mayer and the police found him crying and clawing and punching my father's chest. Two strong-armed firemen had to pry him off. Hold him back. My father identified himself as an EMT, said it was okay, said Mr. Mayer was in shock, and reported the details as he knew them in a calm, even voice.

I didn't know this father, whom others thought capable and trustworthy. I didn't know him at all. I stood back, taking it all in, watching him lay Sean, my Sean, on the stretcher. I wanted to scream again but couldn't. Sean's eyes were shut, but his mouth was open. My father bent over, gently closing Sean's lips, tucking the sheet around his head, nodding to the firemen.

No stars to catch this morning, I thought irrationally, and burst into tears. My father led me away, saying that I had seen enough. There was nothing more anybody could do. He'd said the same thing when my mother died. I was angry at him then too, for being practical, for not seeing how my whole world had ended, and how here, it ended again.

Coach Martinez

The principal—and I—decided to forfeit the final game of the regular season.

The season ends with eleven wins, one loss. The forfeit will be taken as a loss. The other school, with a perfect season, goes on to the region-wide playoffs.

I'm supposed to call each player and let them know we will have a team meeting instead of the game. Psychologists, social workers, the principal will be on hand. But for the moment, nothing.

I'd been working on the roster at my desk in the athletic office. The morning was quiet, the smell of fresh-cut grass making me think how much I loved playing ball. After a week of banging my head against the wall about the incident, after all that was unsaid in this school about racism and hate, after all that I hadn't said—because I wasn't going to get on any soapbox, because I was only a ballplayer at heart, because, maybe, I just wanted to get out of here with my reputation intact—all I wanted to think of was the game. I wanted to coach; I wanted to win.

I was anticipating the opposition's fielding and batting potential, concentrating, feeling like we could win even without Jimmy Seeger. I'd play Mayer in cleanup. We'd mix up the outfield. I was sitting here thinking that even with all that had happened, I love coaching kids. There is always the possibility for redemption in sports, but with kids even more so.

But there is no possibility for Sean Mayer now, is there?

Was it only Friday I overheard Mayer in the locker room talking about his and Jimmy Seeger's so-called "beaner-hopping"? It's

171

another word for plain old assault, that's what I wanted to say. He was saying how Seeger was staying strong in the county jail. How everything was cool with the lawyers.

I stormed into the locker room. Mayer should have been in jail too, not in my locker room. A young guy was dead because of his so-called "beaner-hopping."

Everybody was laughing, gathered around this kid. I walked up to his face and said, "Rice and beans? I like rice and beans. You want to come to my house? Some tasty rice and beans there. Any of you losers want to come to my house? Rice and beans, anytime." No one said a word.

Except for Mayer. He said, "Coach?"

I whirled on him. "Don't talk to me, Mayer."

"Am I in first place or no place, Coach?"

"No place." I turned and hurried out of that locker room as fast as I've ever left a locker room.

Mayer stepped away from the crowd. I remember thinking that I didn't want to see him or hear him ever again. If he had to be here in my gym, I'd ignore him. But he cut me off from leaving with a swift move in front of me. "I'm sorry, Coach," he said softly.

"You're what?" I said, loud enough for everyone to hear.

He stared at the floor, at his bare feet.

"Do you think that makes it okay? Sorry and everything is okay? Sorry? Save the sorrys for somebody else."

Now I need to make calls. The principal insisted it was in the district's best interest that I make these calls as soon as possible. Everyone on the team would probably know what had happened

to Sean. That's the kind of town this is. There aren't secrets. Stress
the team meeting. Don't get into any details with the kids if they
answer the phone. That's what she said.

Yesterday, had my final interview at the high school one town
east of here. They officially offered me the head coaching position.

Must write up my resignation. It will be effective at the end of
school, June 26. Open my top drawer for a pen. And there it is.
Laid out flat. It's the University of Florida at Gainesville recommendation form for Sean Mayer to be considered as a walk-on
for the Gators baseball team. It's on fine paper. I have forgotten,
for a moment, that I had it there. Carefully, I slide the drawer
closed and put my head down and cry for the loss, for his mother's
loss, for him and all the boys.

LONG ISLAND NEWS AT 12 NOON FOR SATURDAY, JUNE 11

ANNOUNCER #1: A prayer vigil was held this morning at the Prince of Peace Assembly for Arturo Cortez, the El Salvadoran immigrant who died this past week after being brutally beaten. The vigil was expected to draw several hundred from churches and synagogues across the island. (Video clip: half-empty sanctuary)

VIDEO: Families are so busy these days . . . With soccer and Little League and everything else . . . It's a shame more people of all faiths did not show what I know is in their hearts. (Caption: Rev. Lawrence I. Exeter)

ANNOUNCER #1: Mrs. Cortez, the mother of the victim, was expected to attend but at the last minute canceled her appearance. A statement from her family noted that she was overcome with grief. She is expected to attend the grand jury hearing, which is scheduled for this week at the county courthouse. There, she will face her son's accused killer for the first time.

ANNOUNCER #2 That's going to be some face-to-face.

VIDEO SCROLL: Breaking News

ANNOUNCER #1: One of the boys accused in the murder of Arturo Cortez has been found dead. The cause of the death is under investigation.

ANNOUNCER #2: His identity is being withheld. But sources close to this case are saying that he was the "mastermind" behind this brutal attack and that he may have acted alone. The "mastermind" behind the Cortez case found dead—breaking news—only from your source for all Long Island news. If it's happening on Long Island, you will find it here.

ANNOUNCER #1: We'll be sure to keep you up-to-the-minute with all developments, so stay here . . .

ANNOUNCER #2: . . . and stay tuned for other news around the island, including your Sunday roundup of high school sports. Coming up next.

ANNOUNCER #1: It's going to be a beautiful weekend on the island to play some ball.

ANNOUNCER #2: Sure is. So stay tuned with us. Long Island News is your place for sports on your island. The complete rundown of sports from high schools across Long Island coming up next.

I am focused only on seeing Jimmy.

I'm not seeing the bulletproof glass. The three guards. I'm sliding my driver's license and birth certificate under the glass. He studies them. I was born here. Long Island. Five minutes from here. But I don't belong here.

One of the guards shakes his head, looking from my zombie driver's license picture back at me. I panic. "It was my birthday this past week. I'm eighteen."

He pushes my driver's license and birth certificate back to me. "Prisoner name?"

"James Seeger."

No reaction, none at all. He makes a note, hands it to the next guard, who checks it and hands it to a third in front of a computer screen, growling under his breath at every request. I'm not sure why there are three guards. Three men with thick necks and jowls side by side like a surly three-headed guard dog, which makes me think, for some reason, of Sean. I can't help thinking of him and the tree and—

"Pay attention, girl," someone whispers behind me, someone in spiked heels and a short, short skirt and long tan legs, someone who likes perfume in heavy doses. "Pay attention, or I'm going ahead of you. I don't got all day."

"You tell her, Claudia," says another voice.

The line is long. I have been inching forward for the past forty-five minutes. It's almost 12:30 p.m. I was here early. I pull my sweater around me. I'm wearing a black tank and a pair of jeans that smelled clean this morning. I brushed my hair off my face. I even found some ChapStick in my mother's drawer. I should have worn lipstick, like her, Claudia. Look-at-me, kiss-me, siren-red lipstick.

"What you looking at with those green eyes? She looks like a cat, a scrawny, hungry cat, don't she? And I hate cats." She breathes this down on my head. Everyone else looks away, bored or wearied or worn down to their bones, even the children.

"Let's move it, ladies and gentlemen. Keep the talking for inside," says another guard, a fourth, ferrying us on.

"You heard the man, keep on moving, girl." She points me to the left. "I see this is going to be one of those days where I got to do everything for everybody."

To the left. Stay in line. Open your backpack. No bottles with broken seals of any kind allowed. No containers more than six ounces. Hand over your half-drunk water bottle. You open and close your ChapStick. Stay in line. Wand check.

"Raise your arms," orders a female guard with feathered hair and bad skin. "Raise them high. Higher."

You're not seeing any of this. You're seeing only Jimmy, soon. Nothing else. You are working through a problem from the calculus test, the one you left blank, involving the definition of continuity and continuous functions. It's yours and yours alone to figure out. Nobody else in this line could work their way through it, that's for sure. If you could do it over, you'd get it right, you're sure.

"Higher. Wake up, girl. The guard said high, that means high."

And you raise your arms up high.

Soon you are inside the packed visitors' room. The walls are lined with posters, one for a hotline for HIV testing, another for domestic abuse, and you stop reading. The room is the size of your high school's lunchroom, with long tables too, except these tables stretch from one side of the room to the other. And instead of rambunctious students, there are men in orange jumpsuits, their prison uniforms, hunched all on one side. You think it should smell like the lunchroom, but it doesn't. A woozy stench of disinfectant, strangely unclean, hangs in the air. Windows are high above you, at ground level. They are narrow, shut tight. An industrial-sized fan blows a hot breeze across the room. Someone groans that the air-conditioning is broke again.

Nobody tells you what to do. You want to think that it's just like the first day of school. You have to find your group of friends. You have to look for Lisa Marie. Except that it isn't school. And none of your friends are with you.

You have to approach a guard. You don't know where to sit, if there are assigned seats. There are twelve guards, one in front of each table. You can't do it. You feel stupid. Defenseless. You feel like you are swimming through air. A door unbolts, clanks, slides opens as if with a groan and sigh. You hear it, and shudder, before you see that that door is the most important door for you to watch. One prisoner, not Jimmy, enters. Ankles are handcuffed. Arms are free, for most, you quickly notice. Each prisoner wears a badge with a number and date and time of entry on his orange jumpsuit.

"Take a seat," orders one of the guards. You realize that he's talking to you, that you are still swimming through air.

You quickly sit down—next to her, siren lips, Claudia. She ignores you. She opens up her blouse two more buttons and everything springs forward, including tattoos of a bird, a wreath of flowers, a heart, and *peace* and *love* in script across the ample space. You don't mean to look, but you do, and she sees, and throws you a kiss. This isn't like school at all.

A murmur buzzes around you. Across every table, people are whispering to one another. One orange jumpsuit, then another, wades through the door.

You've never been good at waiting. The few times you brought your mother to the oncologist, you couldn't bear the waiting room. You'd drive around until she phoned, her voice faint and ragged and asking where you were, and you were nowhere.

You shut your eyes. You have so much to talk about with Jimmy. You need to focus on that. How can you tell him that Sean, of all people, of everyone they know, killed himself? He's going to be devastated. You have to tell him, of course. It changes everything.

And then you're cold, inside, at your core. You're shaking. You're squeezing your eyes shut against the morning's sight. Sean. The tree. You pull your sweater into your chest, and next to you, Claudia's asking out of the side of her lips, "Are you okay, girl? It gets easier. For the past year, ever since I turned eighteen, I've been coming here by myself too. It gets easier."

You're not okay. You're cold and shaking and Sean is dead, and you don't want it to get easier, you don't want to get used to this, and then that door clanks and sighs again and you open your eyes. You see only him.

"I'm fine," you reply. "I'm fine now. There's Jimmy."

Jimmy claims a space at the end of the table. He grins at me, motions for me to join him as if he's been saving the spot across from him just for me and we're going to have lunch, head to study hall or out on the fields. I'll watch him practice. The sun will shine down on us.

"What are you waiting for?" Jimmy asks. His voice hits my heart. I see only him. His blue eyes are bluer somehow. He sits even more square-shouldered, straight-backed. Maybe it's the bright orange jumpsuit that makes him seem even taller or bigger, or both.

His eyes leap up and down me. "Take off that sweater. Please."

I pull my sweater off and tie it around my waist. My arms and neck are bare. "Come on over," he says impatiently. "I miss you so much, Sky, and we just have an hour."

I slide over to him. I want him to lean in to me, want to feel his breath on my skin. I want him to hold me. But he can't. Not here.

"All I want to do is look at you," he says.

"We have a lot to talk about—"

"All week I've been doing visualization exercises. Coach Martinez thinks that I never listen to him, but I've been in that cell and I've been visualizing."

"You have?"

"Yes. You. And the future. And I've been visualizing winning the game tomorrow."

"The game?"

"Mainly you, Sky."

"Oh," I say faintly.

"My grandmother's paying for a pretty sharp, very high-priced lawyer. He's very optimistic. I love that woman. My grandmother. She wouldn't post bond. She has the idea that this place will teach me a lesson. I don't need to learn anything in here, believe me. But she's got me a good lawyer—"

"Everything's changed, Jimmy—"

"What's changed?"

His fingers play with the inside of my arm. I sway toward him. I feel his breath flutter on my neck. The guard, spotting us, wags his finger at Jimmy. Jimmy grins, withdrawing his hand slowly. "That CO is a good guy. A really good guy, if you know what I mean."

"I don't know—"

"But you won't hear me calling him 'sir.' I reserve that for the COs who don't deserve my respect."

"CO?"

"Correctional officer," he says, grinning at knowing something I don't—just like Jimmy. "And I'm glad I can't touch you in here." He is whispering now, and I'm struggling. I need to tell him about Sean.

"Why?" I say. All I want him to do is hold me.

"I need you to stay safe."

"Safe?"

"Look around. Look who's in here." He hunches forward then. "The scum of the earth." And he stretches back. "I don't want to say nothing else."

"I am seeing only you, Jimmy."

He sits back up straight. His eyes bore into mine. "Good. But you and me know that there's another reality. And I don't want to have any trouble in here. My lawyer told me that I got to lay low in here. I can't say anything that would hurt anybody's feelings. But I never do, do I, Sky?"

"Jimmy," I say, shifting in my seat, rubbing my arms, "I have to tell you something—"

"First let me tell you something," he says, folding his hands on the table between us. I always loved his hands, twice the size of mine, full of strength and power and sureness, and I cut myself off. Jimmy. I'm Jimmy's girl. I don't want to think of last Saturday night. I don't want to see anything but Jimmy across from me. "I'm going to make it up to you. I am. I'm sorry. I'm sorry about missing your birthday. I don't have anything for you now, in here. I was going to give you an incredibly special gift. A ring."

"My birthday?"

"It was your birthday yesterday. I didn't forget."

"My birthday was three days ago. Wednesday."

He looks at me like that is the wrong answer, like I've screwed up.

"I'm not thinking of my birthday," I quickly answer. "Something's happened, today, and I don't know how to tell you—"

"Sean."

"You know?"

"My lawyer called me this morning."

Hot air from the fans hits my face and somehow I'm cold, shivering.

"Listen to me, Skylar. Listen. This doesn't change anything for us. Are you okay? How can you be cold? Did you eat today?"

"I ate," I mumble, a white lie. When would I have time to eat? Before or after I found Sean in the tree? And why when a lie is small is it a "white" lie?

I need to talk about Sean, about what I saw. "He was my oldest friend," I say, my voice strangling. "I know you and him became best friends this year. But I've known Sean all my life. I loved him—"

"You have to listen. This doesn't change anything between you and me. In fact, that ring, it's a beautiful ring. It has a pearl at the center, a pure white pearl. It's in my grandmother's safe-deposit box. But it's mine. It's more a friendship ring. It's only for right now. Listen, Skylar, I don't know why Sean killed himself. I don't want to say anything bad about the dead. But he was a moron. An idiot. We pled not guilty; I'm not guilty. And now, between you and me, I have an even stronger case. We—well, my lawyer, not me, was worried about Sean, about what he could say. Maybe he did us a favor, that's what my lawyer said, not me. Now, it's my word against a seventeen-year-old Mexican dropout."

"He's from El Salvador."

"Sky."

"And he was born here."

"Listen, they found pot and a knife on the guy. I was defending myself. And I was. That's what this whole thing was about—making sure you, and me, and Sean and Lisa Marie and everyone else, were safe—making sure my little brother could grow up in a safe place."

"They were brothers too." I rub my arms. Down at the other end, Claudia is dangling across the table. Her tattoos are on full view for her orange-suited companion. He whispers to them like he's telling secrets to the tattoos.

Jimmy looks too, amused at what I'm so interested in. He leans over to me. "You're so much better than her."

I know he means it as a compliment, and at one time, an hour ago, I would have taken it in that way. I jump in my skin. The guard is shrieking his whistle, storming down to the other end of the table. "You know the rules. No physical contact. Get up. Let's go."

Jimmy gives them a bored last look and turns back to me. It takes a moment before Claudia buttons up her blouse. Her hands tremble. She wipes her lipstick off, pressing her palm against her mouth as if it could muffle her anger or grief, I'm not sure which. She's watching her boyfriend being led away.

Jimmy tenses. He perches at the end of the bench ramrod-straight. I need to focus only on him.

"What about Lisa Marie, is she okay?"

"What do you mean?"

"Didn't she grow up with Sean too? Tell her I asked about her. I don't want people to forget me."

"She's worried about what she's going to wear to the funeral. She suffers from a 'lack of black,' as she said."

He laughs. "Then she's okay."

I study him. "Did anything ever go on between you and Lisa Marie?"

"No."

I wait for him to say more beyond no, to flinch, or glance away from me. Instead, his blue eyes bore into mine. He says nothing more. So I go on, carefully. "Actually, we cried in each other's arms all morning. Her mother and father had to pull her away from me. Had to give her something to calm her down. I didn't want anything. A pill, I mean. I was seeing you. I want to be able to think clearly now. I mean, why did Sean kill himself if everything was going to be fine?"

"Skylar, he was my friend too. I didn't mean to be so harsh on Sean. You know that's not me; it's this place. I thought we were going to be buddies for the rest of our lives. The kind of guys that in twenty, thirty years were still playing baseball together, or maybe softball by then, that's more an old man's game. But you know what I mean. I'm sad too. I've lost something too. I wish I could have been strong enough for him and me. I wish I could have done what had to be done. Now I'll carry it all with me. For the rest of my life. I'll never forget Sean."

He says the last part so gently, do I need to hear anything else?

"Listen, Skylar," he continues, barely moving his lips. "I just want to make sure that you are on board. I know you probably had to talk to the police once, but you don't have to speak to them again, at least not voluntarily. You don't."

"I'm not."

"Everybody in the school knew the deal, everybody wanted to be part of it. Doesn't that tell you something?" He flicks his head away from the CO. "I know that you didn't follow protocol that night, Sky."

My thoughts jump. *I just wanted to be with you. I didn't see anything,* I want to lie. I want that to be the last lie. "Please, Jimmy. Please. I told the police that I wasn't there. I only spoke to this one officer, Officer Healey. He asked if this was part of a pattern of attacks, and I said I didn't know. I mean, I said no, it wasn't, that I never heard you say anything derogatory about—"

"Loose lips sink ships, Sky."

"What?" I try a smile.

He isn't smiling. Mine is fake, I know. My hands are ice-cold. I blink; he doesn't. "Don't say more. Not now. Not here. Not ever." He takes a deep breath. Blue eyes sear into mine. "I love you, Sky. Remember that first night we met? Remember the bird? I always think about how I saved that bird. We saved that bird together. You're like that bird to me. Fragile. Your mother said something about birds, I always remember you sharing it with me."

"About feathers."

"That's right. It was a poem from Emily Dickinson. 'Hope is the thing / with feathers . . .' what's the rest?"

I lean in, offering him the next line.

His eyes narrow. "It doesn't matter. Not now. But you always thought that your mother would have liked me a lot, didn't you? I always wish I had met her."

"Me too."

His voice dives. "Listen."

The fans whoop at every rotation. A child cries somewhere. A hand slaps the table. Feet shuffle, chained. I sit very still, my hands at my side.

"Listen," he says, "I need to hear you say that you love me, Sky, that when this is over we'll be together. We'll do just as we planned. We'll take a year off. We'll have our big night. It may not be graduation night, but it will be our graduation night, together, if you know what I mean. We'll sail my grandmother's boat down to Florida. I'll enlist. You'll go to school near where I'm stationed."

"I haven't told my father about not going to college next year. Not yet."

"Skylar, you aren't listening or you're not hearing me."

I am listening with all my heart, but I don't know what he's saying about graduation and his grandmother's boat. I feel like it's my father asking me what I want for breakfast the morning after my mother died. Did I want pancakes or eggs? I wanted to cry or scream or run from that house and him. I never wanted to eat again. Most of all, I wanted to talk about her, what she meant to us, how she would always be with us. What I got was eggs or pancakes. I want to talk to Jimmy about what he's feeling in the same urgent, stomach-churning, life-or-death way. I need to know, just for me, not for anybody else, certainly not the police, that he didn't mean it. He didn't mean to kill someone, however it happened. Even more, that he's sorry, that we'll both be sorry for the rest of our lives, and then we can go on.

"I wish you'd say one thing to me, just to me, Jimmy, no one else," I say, surprising myself. My heart races. "You don't have to say it to anyone else—"

"I said I loved you."

Recklessly, I rush out, "Someone was killed, I mean, someone is dead. And Sean. He was your best friend. He was there with you last Saturday night—" I feel like I'm surfacing. My heart is breaking at the effort. It's beating loud enough for Jimmy to hear; it's beating against his cold hard stare.

"Wasn't it you who told me that *sorry* is a meaningless word?"

"That's not what I meant—"

"All those nights I held you," he says urgently, "and that I held back, I held back for you, Sky. I wanted to control the situation, if you understand me. One of us had to be in control."

"Control?"

"I held back, listening to you as you cried about your mother."

"I don't think I need anyone to control me."

"Protect you, then. That's what I mean. I was your protector, wasn't I? I was there for you, wasn't I? All I ever wanted to do was to keep you safe. I thought you believed in what I believed. You believed in us, didn't you? I need to hear *you* say that, at least."

Over his shoulder, the fan beats. Other couples bend toward each other as if eating one another's words. I believed him, I did. I mean, I believe him. I breathe, blink, surfacing and—

"Hold me with those green eyes. I've been seeing those green eyes in my dreams, Sky."

I can't avoid looking at him, though a stray thought runs through my brain: Jimmy's been sleeping in here; Sean said he couldn't sleep at all this past week. Jimmy's deep-welled blue eyes lock on mine. I feel hopeless, I mean, hopelessly connected to him.

"I'm sorry," he says. "If that's what you think you need to hear? *I'm sorry.* Are you listening to me, Skylar?"

"I'm listening, Jimmy." I am. Sean is dead and someone named Arturo Cortez is dead, and my stomach is tightening, and I'm listening—but somehow that's not exactly what I needed to hear.

His eyes won't leave mine. "Good," he says. "Sometimes I think you've been sleepwalking this entire past year, and I've had to do all the thinking about the future. I'm never letting you go, Skylar, so I need you to understand me. I have a philosophy of life, a personal field manual, and if you had been listening, you'd remember, it's a very simple but effective one—"

"Seeger!"

Jimmy raises his chin slowly, acknowledging the guard, a different one, a Hispanic surname on his badge.

"Yes, sir?"

"Time up."

"Yes, sir."

"Now, Seeger."

"Yes, *sir*."

Across from me, Jimmy rises.

I remember: I haven't said what I truly came to say. When is it too late to say I love you?

Someone has planted petunias in my mother's flower bed.

Seeing them stops me cold. Purple Wave. Fantasy Pink Morn. Yellow Shockers. My mother named her petunias. I run into the house.

I spent the end of the afternoon, after seeing Jimmy, driving, nowhere, again. This time, I saw nobody.

I drove, thinking of Jimmy, of what he said, not what I didn't say, thinking that he's right. This is a small island.

And I have to leave.

I'm using the hundred dollars in birthday money and going. I have more money in the bank when I need it. I'm leaving Long Island. If I'm not here on Monday, I can't talk to the police or any-one. I can get in the Mustang and drive west, straight through the heart of Manhattan. I don't have to stop. I've never driven in the city. I don't care if I get lost. I have nowhere to go. I just have to go.

These are not irrational thoughts. I am amazingly clear-headed. For the first time in a long time, I know what I have to do. I have to pack. Not a lot. Some jeans and T-shirts. A few photos of Jimmy, and of my mother, of course.

But first I have to find one thing of my mother's to take with me. And I have to go back into my father and mother's bedroom. I haven't been back in there since the night she died.

I fling open the door.

The bed isn't made. My father's EMT uniforms, underwear, and socks are scattered across the room. The closets are wide open. Her clothes, even her kimonos, have been pulled off the hangers, lay curled on the floor. Her side of the bed, the right-hand side, is cluttered with a box of tissues, some used, her red reading glasses, and the boa with pink feathers that appeared around her neck after she returned home from chemo for what would be the last time.

We should have thrown it all away. We should have abandoned this house, nailed shut this room, moved.

I bang open the nightstand's drawer, gasping. Lavender, her favorite scent, escapes. I drop to my knees on the bare wood floor, thick with dust bunnies, and search under the bed. I spot what I've been looking for, wedged between the bed and the wall, the oversized paperback six inches thick, the cover bent and torn and Scotch-taped, so many pages marked and highlighted and bent at the corner. I steal it. When I stand up and turn, the book pressed to my chest, there he is, my father, hands and wrists and elbows brown, caked with dirt.

"I'm going."

"No, you're not," he says, surprising me. "What are you doing? What did you do in here?"

"I'm just going to my room."

"You're not going anywhere. What do you have there?"

"I have to go."

I hug the book close. "It's mine," I lie. I'm not saying anything else. I'm not. I'm going. I'm leaving. I may have been sleepwalking, Jimmy was right, but I'm not now. I'll contact the school and have them forward my diploma. I'll pass all my classes even without taking the finals. I'll miss Sean's funeral, though. I look around. I'll miss a lot of things. But whatever happens to Jimmy, it won't be because of me.

I try to push past my father. He blocks my way. "That police officer called me. He said he spoke to you?"

"I'm not volunteering anything to the police."

"I'll stand by you, Skylar. Whatever you say, whatever you do. But I got to tell you, your mother would have wanted you to tell the truth, tell what you saw. That's what I've been thinking."

"If they subpoena me, I'll be there."

"Lookit, your mother was a better person than me. I got to tell you, she had a lot of hope for the future, for my future and yours, and the future in general. She wasn't afraid of anything." He chokes up. "The wrong parent was put in the ground. What can I tell you? I can't tell you anything but this: I love you, Skylar, and whatever you do I'll be there for you. But I hope you decide to tell what you know and leave it to a judge and a jury to decide the rest."

"This is a small island."

"What the hell does that mean?"

All afternoon I've been thinking about what Jimmy said, all the things he said these past months, about our town, our small island. Those are his ideas, not mine, and I don't know what it all means. But I didn't even think before today about what they meant. Once we're together, really together again, we can talk, and I can truly listen. I shrug. I don't know what it means—I have to go, that's all.

My father swipes his hand across his eyes, streaking dirt, pulling himself together a little. I back up. "It may be a small island, and it may be an even smaller world, but that doesn't mean you don't figure out a way to live on it with everybody else. It don't mean you go out and make your own rules, does it? Lookit, I'm not a philosopher or nothing. I just drive an ambulance. But I've been doing a lot of thinking—"

I back up farther until I'm forced to sit down on the bed, on her side, her book still with me.

"Are you tired?" he asks. "You want to take a nap for a while?"

All I can think is that I am sitting on my parents' bed, on my mother's side of the bed, and that I am a little afraid.

"I'm not tired at all. I know what I'm doing. I can't stay here." I smooth my palms nervously across her silk comforter, across its riot of cherry blossoms on black. "This is where she died."

"I know."

I roll my knuckles across the silk, inhale her lavender. The silk is cool. For once, I'm not cold. The thought comes slow and clear. She asked me to tell her the truth. She asked me if she could die, as if she were asking permission; she wasn't. The question was asked so I could answer it. She knew I needed to answer it.

"I was an idiot." From the doorway, my father's voice, full of sorrow, stops me from sliding down upon the silk. "I couldn't do it, though. I couldn't be here at the end, and I should have been stronger or braver or something—"

"That night she died, when she asked me if it was okay—" I say distinctly, wanting him to listen.

He flinches.

"It doesn't matter that you weren't here."

Scraps of his hair stick out the side of his head. He runs his dirt-dried fingers through them and over his head and brow. He's innocently covered with dirt. "Lookit, I wish I could change this past year. I wish I were there for her, and for you. If I had done things different, maybe you wouldn't have hooked up with someone like Jimmy." He glances at me sideways. "You saw him today?"

I hesitate before saying quietly, "Yes."

"Was it what you expected?"

"No. But that doesn't change what I think I should do," I say, with more defiance than I feel. I can't volunteer information to the police. I have to go—

"His father's been calling, wanting to know how the visit went, wanting to know if you were planning on talking to the police again on Monday—"

"I can't talk to him. I mean, I'll talk to Jimmy. But I can't talk to his father again. It's nothing against his father—" I jump up, off the comforter, aim to leave the room.

"Lookit, you can lie to everyone, even to me, even to yourself, but I got to tell you, a lie like that will follow you the rest of your life." He grabs my arm to stop me from passing him and then drops it just as quickly. "I thought if I didn't see her dying she wouldn't die. I should have been there. I should have faced the truth—"

"I can't. If I face it, I'll lose everything."

"You won't lose me." He looks at me, directly at me, like he hasn't in a long time. He has that same calm gaze that he had this morning with Sean and Mr. Mayer. He looks like he can handle almost anything. But I know he can't. He couldn't handle my mother's death.

I cross my arms over my mother's book and stand very still. He shifts from foot to muddy foot. My eyes can't meet his. "I don't want to lose me."

He nods, red in the face. I wish we could just sit and watch the ball game together like we used to, me, six or seven, on his lap, falling asleep before the seventh-inning stretch. There has to be a game on, there always is. He strains to keep looking at me. I realize that he's afraid that he could lose me too.

"There's been so much talking—you, Dad; Lisa Marie." My voice catches. "Jimmy."

Take a deep breath.

"I have to think of what I should say—or not. This is my life. Nobody else's."

That's the only truth I know right now. This is my life. I'm scared, more than a little, having said that. I lean my shoulder against the doorway as if I could fall.

My father considers this, smudging his hand over his mouth. "Lookit, are you hungry? We could go to the diner?"

"No."

"I could make us some eggs? Over easy? With toast? I even got some vanilla ice cream. I could make up some milkshakes to go with it? I know it's not much of a dinner."

I am hungry. Even more than hungry, I want to eat. I give him an okay shrug, which is enough of a yes to have him jump back in excitement.

"You know there's something in that book you're holding that your mother always liked to read to me, as if I knew what it meant."

"You know this was her book?"

"Okay, here's the thing. She tried to get me to memorize a couple of poems in that book of hers you have."

I hold the book tighter. *My book.*

"Forgetaboutit. All I ever got was the first part of one in my head." Before I can say, *Stop, no,* he stands up straight like he's at attention, or a schoolboy being very good.

He sucks in his gut and scrunches his eyes shut. "Hope is the thing / with feathers—"

I'm facing him, startled. It's as if I can hear the sound of my own body. The push-and-drag of my pulse. Something within being struck down by a feather.

"I never got the feather thing. Hope, to me, is something rooted. Planted deep. But what the hell do I know?"

I find my voice. "What about the rest of the poem?"

"Lookit, I forget the rest. Maybe I can start dinner and you can read it out loud. Did you know your mother liked to read that stuff to me? That's the truth. I had to tell her I was being true to myself when I said I'd rather just watch the Mets game. But it was never all her or all me. I got so much to talk with you about, Skylar. I'm starting to think about the future again, for me, for you, for us. And something else, something I got to say before you run off, I'm sorry that kid died. I mean it, now. I'm sorry."

"Sean, I know, I still can't believe this morning." I shudder. *It's never going to be over. Maybe I do need to just go? I could go tonight after he leaves for work—I could just go—*

"I'm sorry to hell about him too. And I'm sorry for his father. And mother. But what I mean is that I'm sorry about what happened to that Arturo Cortez. I'm sorry for his family. For the brother. For his mother. Aren't you?"

Again, I realize I haven't really known this man, this father of mine. He gazes on me with sorrowful brown eyes. I don't think I ever realized that they were also kind eyes. "Did you see his mother on the news?" he says. "She got off that plane from God knows where, thinking that her son was still alive, and *bam*. Must have hit her like I don't know what. A bat in the face." He pauses, gulps for air. "What do you do as a parent, hearing something like that? Your kid is dead from a beating with a baseball bat, over what? Over nothing, that's what I say. Sorry isn't enough, is it?" He blinks, a furious sequence. I feel frozen cold.

"She hated that word—" I say, because I have to say something, and look away. "Mom, I mean. She hated *sorry*."

"*Sorry*? Don't I know it. She hated regretting things, so she never regretted anything, at least that's what she said to me. And she hated even more when people said they were sorry and didn't mean it. She was tough. But absolutely true to herself."

Who am I being true to?

"Lookit, I've been thinking, and you may not want to hear this, but I've been thinking about this all week, and I got to say it, you can't lie about what you know."

"I don't know what I know."

"I think you do," he says. "If you lie, and nobody is found responsible for that boy's murder as a result, you won't know who you are, Skylar. I won't know you are."

"If I'm subpoenaed—"

"You have the opportunity to come forward now."

"I got to go." *I don't want you to know me,* I want to shout. *I don't know me anymore.* "Dad, please."

"You can go, Skylar. Go. Go wherever you got to go tonight. Are all the kids meeting up because of Sean? I figure that's why you were looking for that book. So go. We can talk more later, if you want. I'll wait up for you." He pauses, stops shifting from foot to foot, slumps against the wall.

Neither of us moves. When I said *go,* he thought I meant for a few hours. I don't correct him.

I look at him like I haven't in a long time, which means I don't look at him like I wish he was dead instead of my mother. I look at him and remember he had a way of holding my mother and me together. We'd be watching the ball game. I'd be pressed against his chest hearing his heart beat on one side and my mother would be on the other side, and his arms would tighten tirelessly around us both. He'd stink of sweat and the city, and my mother would smell of lavender.

"Lookit, you know what I did today? I planted flowers. Did you see them? The petunias?"

"You?" I act surprised because he's so pleased with himself. "You should water them."

I push past him, and go.

Hope is the thing
with feathers—
That perches in the soul—
And sings the tune
without the words—
And never stops—at all—

First stanza of poem by
EMILY DICKINSON

Posted by Skylar Thompson on
Sean Mayer's memorial Web page

On Saturday night, I didn't go anywhere but Dunkin' Donuts and cried on the shoulders of Lisa Marie and Jake and Benny and then went home. Today, Sunday, I watered the petunias with my father before he took off for his shift. Finally, it's evening and no one is around.

Sean's dad finds me, or I find him. I shouldn't be here. I should be gone.

And I'm out of here tonight.

Though now I'm under Sean's tree. Sean's dad clanks out of his back door. A whiff of popcorn follows him before the door slams shut. At first I expect he's going to be angry at me. But he gives me a wan, goofy smile. He drags himself around the base of the maple, stroking its bark.

"I remember when Sean asked me to hang that tire in this tree. He said this was 'his' tree. None of the girls had ever asked for such a thing. But, sure, why not? Anything for my son."

He scans the tree branches. This is a grand old tree. Someone has cut down the rope. The branch on which Sean swung is gone too, sawn off. The tree looks sad.

"Skylar," he says, "you know Sean was going to cut a deal. Did you know? I was pushing him toward it. I wanted him to tell the truth. I didn't care what truth. I just didn't want my son to go to jail or to have to check the 'Yes' box on the 'Did you ever commit a felony?' question on a job application."

"Why?" I spread my hand across the tree's rough bark. "Why did this happen? Is our town so different?"

"What are you talking about? It's not different at all. It's a great town. Sean didn't know what he was doing. He didn't know. And all I know is that I didn't want my son to be the boy described in the news. Some kind of racist. Some kind of hater. My son didn't hate anybody. He was too much a follower, not enough a leader. I always said that to him. That was the problem. I would have done anything for him. He should have known that. Skylar, what are we going to do?"

I think he means who will be the one to say what Sean was going to say? Who is going to speak the truth now?

"What am I going to do?" he says with muted anger. "Everyone knew me as Sean's dad. I was Sean's dad, that's all. I did everything I could for him."

He stops circling the tree. "His mother and sisters say they can't bear this maple, this witness."

He throws himself against the tree as if he could rip it from its roots. He screams. Wind ripples across us, carrying the damp night smell of grass and trees and flowers. I think his wife or daughters will run out, but no one does. They must have gone somewhere else to mourn.

Sean's father doubles over in pain. With a flood of fresh tears, he cries out, "Do I have to cut down his tree?"

I lay my arms awkwardly around his shoulders. His grief is so large. I'm stunned, silent, realizing mine is too—for Sean and his family, for Arturo Cortez and Carlos too, for my mother, and my father. Even for Jimmy.

In the Mustang. Midnight. No moon.

A worn-out road map is open on the seat next to me, the kind of map that is impossible for anyone to fold back up, except my father. The entire Northeast of the United States is spread out, though frayed at the creases. The main roads splayed in red or blue, like an old man's veins.

On long car trips, my mother would sit in the passenger seat with a map like this, maybe this one—why do I remember it as new?—laid on her lap. She'd lead us to the place we were going, Maine one year, Florida another. She was always sure there was something interesting right up ahead; she made us stop at every rock with a plaque or overlook with trees and mountains. She made us look.

But then, she believed it was possible to have truth and beauty in the world; even at the brutal end, she recited poetry. It doesn't mean anything, does it?

Tonight, I'm going south, or north, maybe to Boston.

I run my fingers through my hair. It's all strings and knots. I pull at my tank top. I should have worn something other than black.

I'm parked between my house and the Mayers'. Night drapes their home. They've all fled—from the firemen, the police, the reporters, the neighbors, and each other.

Across the street, Lisa Marie's lawn is lit up, same as always. I should go say good-bye to her. But she'll understand why I had to go. I can't face her anyway.

I can't face anybody.

Most of all, I can't face my father. I can't meet him at the police station in the morning. I can't. I'm useless and hopeless.

At least, I know that by not saying anything, I won't hurt anybody else. I especially won't hurt my father anymore. I wish I was more like Lisa Marie, able to live comfortably within a lie, or "remodeled truth," as she put it.

I wish I had said one true thing to Jimmy, as we lay in bed together on nights like these when my father was working and we had the house to ourselves. I wish I had said, *Stop holding back, you don't need to for me, I'm not that fragile. Real love won't break me.*

I stare at the map. Shadows slice it. My heart seizes. I can't leave until I can drive without my hands shaking with cold. I'd look strange on this warm night wearing gloves. I sit on my hands. The image of my father with Sean—of Sean in the car with me—of Carlos in the parking lot—of Jimmy, even, with the bat—of Carlos and his mother—images I don't own, but somehow I do, trace my sight. I shake my head violently. I don't want to see them.

The most important thing is to leave. Go. Find a bridge or tunnel and cross it. *Go.* I have to listen to me now. Be true, to myself.

Go.

One last look. The petunias my father planted, and I ended up watering, plum and gold, along the borders of our house, lovely at night. I pruned the roses too.

I know I've been wrong about him. I thought my father didn't know anything. I don't know when he figured things out, when he saw past our own grief toward someone else's grief so well that it scares me. Makes me see, doesn't it, what is true?

Go.

I'm not ready for this, the police station steps. Lookit, I'm winded, out of shape. Fifty-two white marble steps. Same number as a week ago, but seems like a lot longer trek up today.

Yesterday, Skylar said she'd meet me here. I worked the overnight and came here straight from work. Men and women in crisp uniforms cross the plaza and enter the spinning doors with a whoosh. The lawyer suggested I wear a suit even though she knew I was coming directly from the overnight shift. So I'm wearing my funeral suit, and it's tight around the waist and the tie is strangling me. The tie is blue and green with baseballs flying across. I always thought it was a sharp-looking tie. After all, my daughter bought it for me on Father's Day, maybe five years ago, maybe six.

Nine a.m. and the sun is orange-red flat on the horizon right there in front of me. It's getting hot standing here on this plaza waiting for her. I took today and tomorrow off so Skylar and me can have some time together. Charlie is covering with a new guy. I'm going to get an earful about the new guy on Wednesday, I think, chuckling, drawing the interest of a young cop working front door security. I loosen the tie. The suit radiates Old Spice and mothballs.

I better stand out near the edge of the stairs, better for her to spot me as soon as she arrives. I think of yesterday. Sunday. Jimmy's father called me before I left for work, and threatened what he'd do if Skylar talked. I let him rant for a while, I mean it's his son facing prison, but then when it got personal, about bodily harm,

I hung up on him. He dialed back. I hung up. When the phone rang a third time and it was him, I said that I'd get the police on him if he called me or Skylar or showed up, or in any way threatened me or my family again. I said I've seen men stabbed, shot, strangled, electrocuted, struck dead by cars, buses, trucks, and even baseball bats. I've picked up their broken bodies. I've buried my wife. Him and his son were not going to destroy me or my daughter.

Skylar had been in the backyard attempting to prune Renee's rosebushes. When she came back into the kitchen, I told her about the calls, about the way Seeger, Sr., sounded like a two-bit movie mobster, threatening us. I did a little imitation of him and of me going at it, and we had tears in our eyes from laughing. *Lookit,* I said, trying not to cry more as I smelled the roses in her hair like her mother, *neither of us can go back. Lies can take you a lot of places but never back.* I wanted to hold her but couldn't. I was afraid. We were so close and so far from one another. A measureless ocean of space, her mother would've said. So I did nothing.

Lookit—

Red pants suit. High heels. She's bounding up the stairs, our lawyer, Charlie's daughter, Janice, asking me where Skylar is.

I glance at my watch. Maybe she got lost. Maybe she couldn't find a place to park. Maybe she had a problem with the Mustang. Maybe she forgot her cell phone and that's why she isn't calling me back. She's not one to be late. Maybe she changed her mind—

Janice interrupts my thoughts. "Let me go in," she says with take-charge intensity. "Tell them she's running late. I really hope this isn't a problem. Tell me this isn't going to be a problem Monday for me. Like I said, your daughter can and will be subpoenaed if she doesn't show. The prosecutor knows that he barely has a case without her cooperation and, let me tell you, he has been all over me ever since I said yes to my daddy that I would represent your daughter. Why? I'll tell you why. It's the word of a seventeen-year-old dropout with a Hispanic surname against James Seeger, and his high-priced lawyer, without your daughter." She grips my forearm. "Tell me, she will be here this morning?"

I like Janice. And when she sees I don't have an answer, she spares me, and barrels inside.

"I'll wait," I call after she's already spinning through the doors. Lookit, I believed my daughter when she said she wanted to be true to herself. I have nothing else to believe, no future, if I don't believe in her.

I scan out into the distance, across the plaza and parking lots to what once was potato fields and high grasses and open plains. The sun floods the east. I could go inside where it's cooler, but then she would miss seeing me waiting for her. She might turn back. Lose courage. Come on, Skylar. We can't turn back. I'm here. It's a small island. . . .

. . . and then there she is. *Skylar.* Lookit, her hair is brushed back. She's hurrying across the plaza in a deep purple skirt and a crisp yellow blouse. She sees me. She is looking right at me, and me at her. Her green eyes are even more green in the morning sun. We hold each other tight.

Author's Note

LIE is fiction; the characters all sprung furiously from my imagination over a few short months. However, what made me want to write this novel was a spate of hate crimes by teenagers in Long Island, Brooklyn, and rural Pennsylvania, among other places. I researched hate crimes via several sources, one of which was particularly helpful to me, and also is dedicated to promoting tolerance in our communities and in our schools—the Southern Poverty Law Center.

Thank you for reading *LIE*.

Acknowledgments

To extraordinary women Sara Goodman and Rachel Sussman; and professors Linsey Abrams and Pamela Laskin at City College; to all my fellow graduate students, especially Christian Ghigliotty; to Ed, Caroline K., Joy, Jessie, and Debbie for reading so closely; to friends who sustain me: Kim, Susan K., Charlene, and everyone in the book club; to Lorena and her sons, who helped inspire this work; to Mark, Susan, and David, and now, Moshe, Cindy, and Jacob; to Michael and Sara, and Hal and Fran; to my father; and to Richard, always, thank you.

1. *LIE* features ten distinct points of view. Did the presence of so many unique voices impact the way you read the novel? Were you surprised that there were adult as well as teen points of view? What do you think the writer is trying to achieve with multiple points of view?

2. One main character does not have a distinct point of view—who is it? Why do you think the writer omitted this character from a first-person accounting of events?

3. Who was the most intriguing character to you and why? Whom would you want to be friends with if the characters were real people? If you could send one of the characters a message, whom would you send it to, and what would the message be?

4. "Everybody knows, nobody's talking," says Lisa Marie repeatedly in the novel. What does this mean to her? What does this ultimately represent for the other characters? Have you ever been in a situation where you had to struggle with the decision to tell the truth or not?

5. Sean and Jimmy are both on the football and baseball teams. Why is this important to the plot? How does this impact the decisions they make? How are student athletes treated at your school?

6. As you were reading, were you aware that this book was inspired by real events? Does knowing that influence how you read the novel?

St. Martin's Griffin

7. Look closely at the title: *LIE*. Having read the book, does it now have a double meaning to you? Do you think the writer intentionally used this title because of its multiple meanings? What are the multiple meanings behind the title?

8. In every community there are unspoken "rules," which is the case in the suburban town at the center of *LIE*. What are some of the unspoken rules in the town? Have you ever thought about the unspoken "rules" of your community? Have you ever been in a situation where you had to make a decision you knew would be unpopular with your community, parents, or friends?

9. Were you surprised by the novel's ending? What do you think of the decisions made by Skylar, Sean, Lisa Marie, and Jimmy? Would you have made similar decisions?

10. Ultimately, this novel focuses on larger themes: immigration, race, and tolerance in our society. How did *LIE* influence your ideas on these issues?

For more reading group suggestions, visit
www.readinggroupgold.com.